# THE KNIFE
# IN MY BACK 2

STACEY COVINGTON-LEE

www.staceycovingtonlee.com

Cover Design: The Final Wrap

Formatting/Typesetting: Under Cover Designs

ISBN – 978-1-7338811-1-1

Second Printing @ Copyright 2019

Published by SCL Novel Publications

Printed in the United States of America

Stacey Covington-Lee
n o v e l s

*This is for every child that has ever suffered the affects of sickle cell. You are not alone, there is a multitude of us and prayerfully, a cure for all is just around the corner.*

# CHAPTER ONE

One of the prison guards knocked on the warden's office door. He waited a few seconds and when there was no response, he knocked a second time. He hated this watch and having to deal with this situation. He knew exactly why there was no immediate answer, every officer in the prison knew why.

"Who's there?"

"It's Officer Todd, sir. I'm here to escort prisoner 68666 from her work detail to her therapy session."

Officer Todd heard the door lock click and rolled his eyes upward as an outward display of his disgust for the entire situation. He was silent as the door opened to reveal inmate, Tameka Williams, pulling her shoulder length hair back into the pony tail it was in when she had been delivered to the office an hour ago. Tameka caught his eye and gave Officer Todd a wink and little crooked smile. Officer Todd shook his head and said a little too loudly, "that child needs Jesus."

"Did you say something, Officer Todd?"

"No sir, Warden Kemp. Talking to myself I guess."

"Something on your mind?"

"No, sir, just thinking about my upcoming weekend and all that I have to do."

"Well I think Ms. Williams is ready to go now. Would you all please close the door on your way out?"

"Yes, sir."

Tameka stepped out of the tastefully decorated office with its pictures on the walls and oversized couch and into the dull, gray hallway. She closed the door as she stepped over the threshold and looked up at Officer Todd with that same little crooked smile. Officer Todd held out a pair of handcuffs and proceeded to place them on Tameka's wrists. He then lifted his hand in a gesture to point her down the hall. They turned left and headed down the depressing corridor that smelled with the stench of hopelessness and despair. As they walked on, Tameka couldn't help but glance up at Officer Todd every now and then. He was so tall and perfectly built. Indeed a beautiful man whose beauty went far beyond his physical appearance.

"You know, Officer Todd, my offer still stands. I could make you a very happy man."

"It seems to me that you have your hands full keeping Warden Kemp happy."

"I *have* to do that, but you, baby, I *want* to do you."

"Well, thanks for the offer, but as I've told you time and time again, my wife *does* me just fine. She's all I need and want."

"I don't know what that woman has put on you, but she's got you whipped. You sure she ain't got roots on you?"

"Tameka, girl, you are so much better than this. Just because your body is in prison doesn't mean that your mind has to be. You are a college graduate, used to be a news reporter, and now listen to you talking about 'ain't got.' What kind of grammar is that?"

"Oh here you go, preacher man. Why do you always have to talk to me like this?"

"Because I know that you can be better than your circumstance, girl. Yes, you got yourself in here, but you can rise above it now. Don't let these other inmates drag you down into their holes of hell. This is all that so many of them have ever known and all that they want to know. You've known better and done better. And as far as Warden Kemp is concerned…"

"Okay, I've got one therapist, I don't need another. Please stop it with your little sermon. Enough already!"

"Fine, we're here now anyway."

Officer Todd tapped on the door to Dr. Lamb's office and pushed it on open. He stepped to the side to give Tameka room to enter. He pulled out his keys and un-cuffed Tameka's hands. "Be a good girl," he stated with authority. Office Todd smiled at the doctor and eased on out of the room closing the door behind him.

Tameka looked around the room and then walked over to take her usual seat on the chaise lounge. This was the one piece of furniture in this whole depressing place that reminded her of the life she used to have. It was the little bit of luxury she got to enjoy once a week. Tameka lay back and ran her hand over the fabric. What a joy it would be for her to be allowed to sleep here every night instead of on that half inch thick excuse for a mattress she'd been condemned to for the past six years.

"Hello, earth to Tameka. Can you hear me?"

"Yeah, yeah I hear you, doc, but you should know the routine by now. I have to have a couple of minutes to soak up my seat. I have to enjoy it while I can cause when I leave this room, its back to metal chairs and a bed that has a concrete slab as its box spring."

"I would think that after all these years you would have adjusted to all of that."

"Do you think you'd be able to adjust?"

"Hmm, not sure. Guess I'd actually have to be in that situation to give an honest answer. But enough about that, how has this week been going for you?"

"It's been the same as every other week. You always ask me that stupid question like you actually expect a different answer. I got guards telling me when to wake up, when to bathe, when to eat, when to exercise and when to go to bed. You'd think after all this time that you would know the drill never changes."

"Well actually, Tameka, that's a good thing. It means that you're staying out of trouble, staying out of solitary. That's the best thing you can do because I don't know if you realize it, but you only have seven more months before your seven year term is up. You could actually be a free woman in less than a year."

"Of course I realize it! I've been counting every second of my time down. I cannot wait to be on the other side of those prison gates. The thought of freedom excites the hell out of me."

"Does it scare you at all?"

"Why would it scare me?"

"Well, a lot has changed in the past six years. You won't have the same home, the same job, or the same friends. That could all be a little intimidating."

"Wow, way to spread a little despair, Dr. Lamb. You paint such a pretty picture that I may just go hang myself."

"I'm not trying to spread despair or paint an ugly picture, Tameka. I'm just stating the facts, being realistic."

"Well the facts are, doc, I will have the same home because wherever my mom is that is where my home will be. That will never change. I also have Wayne waiting for me. His love for me has never faltered throughout this whole ordeal. I've never really had friends. So you see, doc, some things have remained the same. The rest, well I'll adjust."

"That's a good attitude to have; I must say that I'm a little impressed. So have you given any more thought to what you'd like to explore as a career choice once you're released? If it's something within reason, I can try and get you on a program that will give you some hands-on experience right here in the prison. That way you'll have a leg up once you're released."

"I've been thinking about it, but haven't made a solid choice yet. I would love to be able to do something in the news industry, but I know that that's a long shot."

"I have to agree Tameka; you have to be more realistic. To

say that you've burned some bridges in that field of work would be a monumental understatement. And while we're on the subject, I have something to tell you. Remember Monica Grier, the newscaster you set up and had fired under suspicion of drug abuse?"

"How could I forget that witch?"

"Be prepared, you'll begin to see her in a more high profile role on television soon. She's landed the position of host for the nightly local entertainment show *Atlanta Topics*."

Tameka stood up and started walking around the room, pacing back and forth like some kind of defeated, caged animal. She walked over to the window and pressed her face against the bars that blocked her from the actual glass. All she could think about was all that she had done to try and destroy Monica. She thought of how badly she'd wanted Monica's position as news anchor and all she had to do to actually get it. She had literally ripped Monica's life apart, but it looks like Monica was having the last laugh.

"How does this news make you feel, Tameka?"

"What kind of dumb ass question is that? I feel like crap. I tried to break that woman and instead, I'm the one that ended up broken and behind bars. Monica has moved on with her life and has apparently been made stronger by all that I put her through. The only person I ended up hurting was myself. Aren't I the fool?"

"Absolutely not, you are nobody's fool, Tameka. I never thought I'd see the day when you'd take total responsibility for something you did to harm someone else. But just listen to yourself, listen to your words. They tell the story of how much you've grown and matured in this place. You've obviously learned from your past and that puts you in a great position for a bright future."

"That all sounds good, Dr. Lamb, but it doesn't change the fact that Monica is rolling in dough and I'm living in hell."

"Tameka, your body may be locked up in this hell, as you

call it, but your mind, honey, your mind can be free. Free to learn, free to grow and free to plan for an awesome future."

"You sound like Officer Todd."

"Well, Officer Todd must be one smart man."

The two women chuckled and Tameka resumed her position on the chaise. She would never tell Dr. Lamb, but quite honestly, Tameka was surprised by her reaction as well. There used to be a day when her mind would be set on destroying Monica once again. But how could she be mad at Monica for enduring all that she'd put her through and still coming out on top. Had to give the woman her props. She'd been knocked down, wrongly accused and still got back up to become lead anchor once more and now host of her own show. Maybe she should've been learning from Monica instead of trying to replace her.

The knock on the door disrupted Tameka's train of thought. She sat up and rubbed the fabric once more. Dr. Lamb hit the button under her desk to unlock the door and in walked Officer Todd.

"Our time is up, Tameka, but I look forward to speaking with you again next week."

As the officer placed handcuffs on Tameka, she looked up with a smile, "Okay, doc, we'll talk next week. Enjoy your weekend."

"You too, Tameka, and remember, let your mind be free."

Officer Todd and Tameka quietly walked back to the cell block. When the door slammed shut locking Tameka in once more, she decided to free her mind by thinking of her future, her career, her life beyond this prison.

# CHAPTER TWO

As her time continued to tick down, it seemed as if everyone was trying to bait Tameka into a situation that would screw up her release. Her cell mate, Kari seemed to be fighting with everyone on the block and was constantly trying to get Tameka to fight her battles. When Tameka refused to get involved, Kari turned on her and decided that she would do what she could to screw with Tameka. The constant taunting and harassment was becoming more than Tameka could bear. She had actually turned to prayer as a way of dealing with Kari and some of the others that wanted to see her time extended. Tameka just wasn't ready to cave to the urge to beat the hell out of someone and mess up her release.

Officer Todd came to take Tameka to her weekly therapy session. As he escorted her through the dingy, concrete halls, he couldn't help but notice that she wasn't her usual smart mouthed self.

"Is there a problem, Tameka? Something going on with you?"

"If there were, what would be the point in my telling you? There wouldn't be a damn thing you could do about it."

"You don't know what I can do, girl. Besides, it may help to talk about it, you know, to someone who won't be jotting down notes as you speak."

"Man, these witches just won't leave me alone. All I want to do is stay clean and out of trouble so I can get the hell out of this crap hole."

"Now you know that if they get wind of someone's pending release date they will do all that they can to make sure that the person stays in here. You've been here long enough to know that these life timers don't want to see anyone else leave."

"I've fought really hard to be cool with everyone on the block. I never thought that they would try and ruin my chance to get out of here. Even Kari is tripping on me. Just won't get off my back."

I told you a long time ago, never forget where you are. You have no friends in here and you can't trust anyone that's confined in this space. You've been doing real well though, haven't let them pull you into anything negative. Try and remember not to do anything that could be held against you when your parole hearing comes up."

"I hear you. I'm doing my best."

"Your best may not be good enough, Tameka. You must stay on your game in order to get out of here. Well here we are, girl. Go on in and make nice with Dr. Lamb and maybe you can see if she will request extra sessions or work detail for you. That will give you less time on the block to get in trouble."

"Thanks, Todd."

"That's Officer Todd."

"Yeah whatever, man."

Officer Todd chuckled and tapped on Dr. Lamb's door. After Tameka stepped into her place of luxury, Officer Todd closed the door and listened for the click to make sure it locked. As he turned to leave, he said a little prayer for Tameka. He had seen such progress in her since she first arrived. He recognized the potential in her and wanted to see her free and making great strides in her life. Truth be told, when Tameka was a news anchor, he had a little crush on her. His wife would tease him often about his "thing for the news girl." Officer Todd felt such pity for her when he watched her arrest and subsequent conviction all play out on the news. It was indeed a long, hard fall from grace.

Tameka made herself comfortable on the chaise. Dr. Lamb noticed that she seemed a little out of sorts, so she gave her a little time to relax before beginning the session.

"What's going on with you today, Tameka?"

"Just trying to maintain until I can get out of here."

"Are you having problems that might interfere with your release?"

Tameka went on to share with Dr. Lamb her previous conversation with Officer Todd. She told Dr. Lamb of the many verbal assaults she had been enduring lately. She spoke of all the lengths that some of the inmates were going to in an effort to try and provoke her. Dr. Lamb asked if additional work details would help her stay out of trouble.

"I don't know if I'm in a place mentally to make myself more available as Warden Kemp's concubine."

"I thought you told me that he hadn't been approaching you in that way lately."

"Well that could all change if I were around him more, I'm sure of it. It's like he goes through these spells of guilt or something for messing around on his wife. But trust me, those spells don't last long and I know if he sees me more often, he'll want me to start being intimate with him again. I just don't think I can handle that and the girls on the block. All I want is to get out of here. These last three months are squeaking by so slowly."

"Tameka, I've been telling you for years, I can have him brought up for disciplinary action if you would come forward. Then you won't have to worry about him bothering you ever again."

"Dr. Lamb, if I wouldn't say anything back then, you know I'm not going to say anything now. I'm too close to leaving. Let his next whore speak up and make a stand against his fat, nasty ass. I just want out."

"Okay, well maybe he'll be feeling generous when I ask him for more sessions to prepare you for your parole hearing. I'll also contact your attorney to see if he can make himself more available. More meetings with him means less time on the block."

"I'd appreciate that, doc."

"Well don't be too appreciative, he hasn't said yes yet. I think I can convince him, but just in case, don't get your hopes up."

"Not to worry, I never do."

"So moving on, Tameka, have you heard from your mom or Wayne lately? Do they plan to speak on your behalf at the parole hearing?"

"I spoke with my mom about a week ago. She said that nothing short of death would keep her away. She was so happy when I agreed to pray with her over the phone. That seemed to have made her more proud of me than anything else I've ever done in my life."

"And Wayne?"

"Now you know he's like the Maytag repair man…dependable as ever. He's been my rock this entire time. He's my something to look forward to. He'll definitely speak on my behalf and show them that I'll have a stable environment to go to."

"Great, that will surely help when we plead for your freedom. Did you ever write that letter to your victim's family asking for their forgiveness?"

"I did, but just like my other letter, I received no response. Why would I expect to? I killed those people's son. Sometimes I wonder how I'll die after the horrible way I caused another's death."

"Back up, Tameka. What other letter are you referring to?"

"The one I sent to Brook. I pleaded for her forgiveness, and I guess I was half expecting a visit or a letter where she'd accepted my apology. Apparently she isn't as forgiving as I thought."

Unable to hide her annoyance, Dr. Lamb began ranting her

disapproval. "I advised you not to correspond with Brook. She has no bearing and no say as to whether you get paroled or not. Why would you not follow my advice? Why would you risk stirring up unnecessary trouble for yourself?"

"I figured it couldn't hurt since she wouldn't be allowed to speak at the hearing anyway. I called myself trying to make a step in a positive direction and mend fences."

"Tameka, you are still carrying far too much baggage and harboring too much resentment with the whole Brook situation. You've made progress, but not enough to reach out to her. And honestly, it makes me even question your motives. Is it really forgiveness you want from her?"

"I'm sorry you feel that way, doc. I have made progress and you'll just have to trust that my heart is in the right place."

# CHAPTER THREE

Standing in the front door sipping coffee, Brook waved goodbye to Eric. She was still so thankful to God for bringing him into her life. They'd now been married seven wonderful years and had two delightful children. Who could ask for more? Brook slowly closed the door and went upstairs to her study. She'd decided last night to work from home today. Actually she could work from home every day and it wouldn't be a problem. Since she and Eric owned the company, who would dare complain about whatever she decided to do? Eric had generated so much revenue for his old company that he and Brook decided four years ago to stop making other folks rich. They invested their money, time and energy into building their own investment firm. It was the move of a lifetime and had paid off handsomely for them.

Brook sat at her desk and pulled out the white envelope with the correctional institute address stamped on it. She looked at the envelope thoughtfully as she had so many times since receiving it. Brook hadn't told anyone about its arrival and hadn't bothered to open it. Her first reaction was to tear it up and throw it in the trash, but something just wouldn't allow her to do that. Maybe it was curiosity that forced her to hold on to the letter. Part of her really wanted to know what Tameka had to say, but another part still wanted to forget that Tameka even existed. But Brook knew in her heart that she could never forget that woman. She could never forget her because she could never forget the precious baby that Tameka took from her. Brook thought back to her first pregnancy and the joy she felt. Then she thought of the pills that Tameka snuck into her drink causing her miscarriage. Brook would never be able to comprehend how jealously could drive someone to do something so evil. No, forgetting Tameka was not an option. Brook grabbed her letter opener and sliced it through the top of the prison envelope. She pulled out the single sheet of paper and unfolded it. She took a long cleansing breath before reading its contents.

Dearest Brook;

I know that you never expected to hear from me and probably would have preferred that I not try and reach out to you. However, there are some things that I had to say and feelings that had to be expressed so that you could fully understand where I am in my life now and how I plan to proceed.

As you can imagine, the last few years have been hell for me. I have had nothing but time to sit and reflect on how I was leading my life and how destructive I was to others. I have come to understand that my entire way of thinking was distorted and wrong. I have destroyed lives that can never be restored. I am so sorry for taking your child. I am sorry for using you and taking advantage of your kindness. I know that it's not enough, but Brook I am truly sorry. If I could take it all back I swear I would. And I know that I have no right to ask you for anything, but please, please try to find it in your heart to forgive me.

You'll be glad to know that I have been in therapy for the past few years and have learned a lot about myself and what is and is not appropriate behavior. I have worked hard and made much progress in my efforts to be a better person. I look forward to my release in the upcoming months and being able to prove to not only myself, but the entire world that I am worthy of being given a second chance.

Wishing you the best,

Tameka

Brook felt such a rage rise up in her. She cursed Tameka's name as she balled the letter up and threw it across the room. How dare the state give her another chance at life when she'd so maliciously taken an innocent baby's life. Brook dropped her head in her hands and began to cry.

Hearing the front door shut, Brook jerked her head up. Eric must have forgotten something. She grabbed a tissue and began wiping her tears, but her emotions were still written all over her face.

"Babe, where are you?" Eric called out.

"I'm in my office. Did you forget something?"

Brook heard Eric running up the stairs and tried to put on a pleasant face. She failed miserably.

"Can you believe I ran out of here without my briefcase? What's wrong with you, baby, why do you look as if you've been crying?"

"I'm fine, Eric, just feeling a little emotional today. Ignore me."

"Impossible to ignore someone as beautiful as you."

"Well aren't you the charmer."

"I try, but back to the subject at hand, what's got you feeling however it is you're feeling? You seemed fine when I left a little while ago."

"It's nothing, baby, besides don't you need to be heading back out to work?"

"I can afford to go in later. What's wrong, Brook? You're keeping something from me, I can tell. What is it?"

Brook pointed to the balled up paper on the floor. "That came a few days ago, but I just opened and read it this morning."

Eric walked over and picked the letter up and began to read. With each word he read, Brook could see the anger boiling within her husband. She noticed his clinched jaw and narrow eyes. Eric hated Tameka with every fiber of his being and his only regret in life was that he didn't strangle her to death when he had the chance.

"When did you get this garbage?"

"I just decided to open it this morning. Now I wish I had followed my instincts and thrown it away when it first arrived. Reading that crap only forced me to open old wounds."

"You should have told me when it first came, Brook. I told you that no form of communication would ever be accepted from that sick ass woman. I need to contact our attorney and see if this is enough for us to be allowed to speak against her at that parole hearing."

"Please, Eric, calm down. We've already been told that we have no place at that hearing. Her incarceration had nothing to do with the things she did to us."

"Well there has to be something that someone can do to keep her from communicating with you."

"I doubt it, baby. Soon she'll be out of prison and will be free to do whatever she wants again."

"I just don't like this Brook; I get a real bad feeling about her reaching out to you. Tameka doesn't care about being forgiven, and she certainly doesn't care about you or anyone else she ever hurt."

"You're probably right."

"No, not probably, Brook. I am right," Eric ranted.

"Well, not to worry, babe. You know, they say the first cut is the deepest and they are right. There's nothing Tameka could do to hurt me more than she already has, and she'll never have the opportunity to get close enough to hurt me again."

Eric pulled Brook into a strong embrace that made her feel loved as well as protected. Brook knew that there were no limits to what Eric would do to protect her and their children. Seeing him this angry almost made Brook fear more for Tameka's safety than her own. What Tameka didn't realize was that Eric would break her in two if he felt it necessary. No, Brook had no more fear for what Tameka could do to her; it was Tameka who had better be fearful if she tried to contact the Banks family again.

After Eric left for the office, Brook picked up the phone and called Mia. Now that she'd calmed down, she couldn't wait to tell Mia about the letter she'd received. Unfortunately, she would indeed have to wait. According to Mia's secretary, she was in a meeting for the better part of the morning, but Brook's message would be stamped urgent.

Brook looked at her watch and realized that the day was getting away from her. She went into the bedroom to straighten up a bit and then moved on to the kid's room. With this little bit of cleaning, she realized that she was spoiled rotten. The housekeeper was only two days into her vacation and Brook missed her terribly. But she knew she had to suck it up and finish the house work, figure out what she'd prepare for dinner, and then go pick up the children from school. A woman's work is never done.

A couple of hours had passed and Brook had just placed her salmon in marinade when the phone rang.

"Hello."

"What's so urgent, Brook?"

"I got a letter from an old friend and thought I'd share it with you."

"This is the emergency?" Mia asked dryly.

Ignoring Mia's annoyance, Brook began to read the letter. She took her time and read it slowly, wanting to make sure that Mia heard every word correctly. Then she waited for a reaction, and wow, that didn't take but a couple of seconds.

"What the hell! I mean, what the hell, Brook! That bitch has some nerve writing a freaking letter. I can't believe that she tried to reach out to you at all."

"I know, neither could Eric and I."

"When did you get this trash?"

"A couple of weeks ago, but I just opened today."

"What did Eric have to say?"

"He was absolutely furious. And, Mia, I'm not concerned with my safety, I'm more concerned with Tameka's if she ever tries to contact me again. Eric swears that he will kill that girl."

"Good, I'll help him."

"You are crazy, Mia."

"Yeah, crazy like a fox. But seriously, I can't believe Tameka's nerve. More importantly, I can't believe that they are actually going to let her out of prison. I wonder if the family of the man she killed will speak out at her parole hearing?"

"No, unfortunately I heard that his mom died about a month ago. I think that she was his only surviving relative in the area."

"So Tameka basically gets a get out of jail free card."

"Looks like."

"There is so much about this entire situation that's just not right. But, Brook, my dear friend, can we pick this conversation up later? I've got to get on this conference call."

"Well I'm done with this particular conversation, but we can certainly talk later. And don't forget about dinner here at the house on Sunday."

"We'll be there with bells on. Later."

# CHAPTER FOUR

Tameka was a little excited about the remainder of her day. She was looking forward to a visit from Wayne and her mother. This would be one of her last prison visits. Tameka's time was winding down and her parole was looking very promising. Apparently, there would be no one from the victim's family to oppose her release, but she still had her mom and Wayne to speak on her behalf. No, it wouldn't be long now before she was tasting freedom.

There was a knock at Warden Kemp's door, and she knew that it was Officer Todd coming to get her for her visitation. She jumped up from her seat and headed toward the door, but she was stopped by the warden just before she could pull it open. He firmly placed his hand over the door knob and looked Tameka square in the eye.

"Baby, don't get too excited. I hadn't let you do your thing lately, but that doesn't mean that your chance isn't coming around soon. Before you leave this place, you will do me right over and over again. I'll need to get my fill of you, enough to keep me going long after you're gone."

He pressed his body against Tameka's and nastily licked the inside of her ear. It was enough to make her vomit, but she suppressed the feeling long enough to get out of the office and safely into Officer Todd's custody.

"How was your work detail today?"

"You know, Todd, it was fine until you knocked on the door. That's when that sweaty pig reminded me that he was going to *let me do him* before my release. These last few weeks will be difficult to say the least."

"You don't have to do that, Tameka."

"You and I both know that I do if I want to get out of here. If I refuse him now, he'll make sure that my chance for parole gets revoked and that I never get out of this place. So I'll just have to do what I have to."

"I'm so sorry, Tameka, you don't deserve his abuse."

"Apparently something in the universe feels that I do deserve it."

As they turned the corner and entered the visitation room, Tameka seemed to forget all about Warden Kemp. She smiled widely as she approached Wayne with open arms. His embrace was so comforting. He was indeed her rock. Seven years in prison and he was still waiting for her, still loving her unconditionally. She stepped out of Wayne's embrace and began looking around for her mother.

"Where is my mom? Did she have to go to the restroom?"

"No, sweetie, she wasn't able to come today. She's been a little under the weather."

"What's wrong with her? She has never been too sick in the past to make her visitation."

"I know, but she's actually in the hospital. It seems that her cold progressed and developed into pneumonia."

"Oh my goodness... I can't believe that she's stuck down there in that nasty county hospital by herself."

"She's not in the county hospital, Tameka; she was admitted into Emory."

"There is no way my mom could afford that, not even with her Medicare. Are you paying for her to be there?"

"Baby, you know that your mom and Brook have remained very close over the years. Apparently Brook was very concerned for your mom when she became ill. She took your mom to a new physician and is picking up the tab for her care."

"So, Brook saves the day…again." Tameka's expression was not one of appreciation.

"Just be grateful, babe, that your mom is receiving excellent care. I did talk to her before I came here and she sends her love. Your mom can't wait to speak on your behalf to that parole board. She desperately wants you out of here."

"Yeah, I can't wait to be with her. I really want to be in a position to take care of her myself. I'm her daughter; I should be the one providing for her."

"You'll have your chance very, very soon."

The remainder of Tameka's visit with Wayne was very enjoyable. They spent their time making plans for the future and fantasizing about her first night of freedom. She could hardly wait for the opportunity to be with a man that actually loved and respected her. She wanted to be with Wayne because she knew that his love for her was real. She was his woman, not his whore. Once she was released, she'd never be another man's whore.

An hour later, Wayne was gone and she was escorted back to the block. Dinner was over and she was now preparing for lights out. Before she could finish putting her personal items away, one of the night guards came to get her. Unfortunately, Warden Kemp had decided to work late and needed her assistance.

She was escorted through the halls in complete silence. But once they were outside the warden's door, the officer grabbed her rear and suggested that she let him be next. Tameka pushed his hand away; she had no fear of him. The only good thing that the warden ever did for her was keep her protected from those lecherous night guards.

Tameka stepped into the office and closed the door. The warden walked up to her, kissed her softly, and clicked the lock;

she was trapped. But something about him seemed very different tonight. He was usually cold and forceful, but now, he was soft, gentle, almost caring. Even the atmosphere was different; it seemed almost romantic. The lights were dim and there was actually music playing. It was barely audible, but yes, it was definitely music.

"Tameka, this is our last time being together like this. I've got to adjust to not having you around anymore. I'm going to miss you."

"Please, warden, we both know that you'll have me replaced within the month. You've just got to take time and walk the blocks to find your new *assistant*."

"You're wrong, Tameka. I'm being moved to a men's facility next month. Besides, no one could ever replace you. All these other women have never been anything and will never be anything. You are different. You're smart, talented and will rebuild your life into something to be respected."

On some level, Tameka was actually flattered. She felt as if he really meant what he was saying. But none of that talk could make up for the years of abuse. Despite the music and lighting, Tameka had no romantic feelings toward this man what so ever.

The warden led Tameka to the couch. He began to kiss and fondle her. With every stroke of her body, he became more aggressive, became the man that she knew him to be. The kindness and gentleness were gone. He pushed her down and forced himself into her. Tameka laid there with tears running down her face and prayed for it to be over soon. And finally, he stopped pushing and collapsed on top of her. She nudged him until he finally rolled off.

How ironic that the warden gets transferred at the same time of her release. If she never knew it before, Tameka realized now that you had to pay for the wrong that you put into universe.

The next day, Tameka was escorted to Dr. Lamb's office for an unscheduled appointment. Tameka couldn't imagine why she had to see the good doctor today. Officer Todd was unusually quiet on their walk to the office, and he even went inside Dr. Lamb's office with her. This couldn't be good.

"What's up, doc? I'm not supposed to see you until tomorrow."

"Have a seat, Tameka."

"I'll stand, what's up? Have they revoked my parole?"

"No, dear. I don't know if you're aware, but your mom has been quite ill."

"Yes, I'm aware."

"Unfortunately, she passed early this morning due to complications from pneumonia."

Tameka passed out cold.

# CHAPTER FIVE

Unexpectedly, Tameka arrived at the church on Wayne's arm. Walking in behind them and taking a seat on the last pew was Officer Todd. Yes, Tameka was supposed to be escorted by police and shackled at all times, but Officer Todd couldn't bring himself to make her mourn while chained like an animal. He and Tameka met Wayne around the corner from the church where he, to Tameka's surprise, unchained her and turned her over to Wayne. Officer Todd was betting his career on the fact that Tameka wouldn't try anything crazy.

Tameka stood over her mother and silently wept. She gently stroked her mom's face and admired her beauty. Her mother was wearing a lovely white dress for her eternal rest. She was lying in what had to be an $8,000.00 coffin that cradled her in soft, yellow satin with praying hands embroidered in the top. As Tameka made her way to the front pew, she looked around with admiration at the dozens of yellow roses and other plants that filled the church. The sanctuary was also packed with friends and family. Tameka was pleased to see her brother making his way down the aisle to view their mother's remains. He stood briefly with his mother and then went to seek comfort in his sister's arms.

As the minister was preparing to begin the service, Tameka spotted Brook and Eric out of the corner of her eye. There they were, looking like the millions that they were worth, making their way to the front pew across the aisle from Tameka. Turning to Wayne, Tameka begin to shake with anger. "What the hell are they doing here?"

"Tameka, look around, who do think paid for this service? You're mother had no

life insurance. You should be grateful."

"I don't understand why she couldn't let me have this time to say goodbye. She has had my mom for the past seven years," Tameka whimpered. Then suddenly with venom in her voice, she glared at Brook and shouted "Can I not have this time without having to be in her presence?"

"Lower your voice and show some respect," Wayne reprimanded. "Like I said, you should be grateful. You know that you would not have wanted some state funded burial for your mother. Brook is honoring your mom's life by sending her out like this."

"Sis, I have to agree with Wayne on this one. You need to chill and be grateful," chimed Tameka's brother.

The service lasted for about forty-five minutes and many wonderful things were said about Lucille Williams. The recessional began, and as they were walking out of the pews, Tameka and Brook were face to face for the first time in seven years. Tameka glared with disdain and marched out of the church. Officer Todd met Tameka and Wayne at the door and escorted them to his patrol car around the corner. Tameka and Officer Todd followed the recessional to the cemetery and of course, Wayne was not far behind.

The internment was brief. As the crowd began to disburse, Tameka thought that a little appreciation might actually be in order and made her way over to Brook and Eric. "Brook, I just wanted to thank you for all of this. Thank you for everything you've done for my mother over the years."

"Your mother was a good woman, she deserved this," stated Eric. Brook never spoke a word to Tameka; she simply turned and walked away.

"So it's like that, Brook?" Tameka shouted at her ex-friend's back. "You can't acknowledge my words, my presence? I'm not invisible," she cried out.

Tameka turned and reached for Wayne. He took her into his arms and comforted her. He kissed her gently and then she moved to her brother's embrace. "I love you guys," she whispered, and then she was escorted away by Officer Todd. They rode for about an hour in complete silence. The only noises were the sniffles that would occasionally escape from Tameka as she continued to mourn.

"We should be there soon, Tameka. When we get a little closer, I'll have to stop and handcuff you, okay?"

"Yeah, I know."

"Do you want to stop and get something to eat?"

"No thanks."

They rode for another thirty minutes before Officer Todd pulled over to the side of the road. He got out and opened the door for Tameka. He proceeded to place shackles on her feet and cuffs on her hands. Before getting back in the car, Tameka stood on her tip-toes and kissed Officer Todd on the cheek. "Thank you for not humiliating me today." She then bent down and wiggled into the backseat of the car.

# CHAPTER SIX

Brook and Eric returned home after the funeral and Brook was so glad that the kids were with Mia for the night. She welcomed the quiet time and immediately went upstairs and changed into something comfortable. By the time she returned downstairs, Eric had prepared her a nice cup of tea. They sat on the couch together and Brook let out a deep sigh.

"Are you okay, baby?" Eric quizzed.

"I will be. I'm going to miss Ms. Williams so very much."

"I know, but I also know that she would be so pleased with her services, and she made no secret of how much she loved you. She really treasured you all's relationship."

"So did I. I'll never understand how such a wonderful woman could have birthed someone as evil as Tameka. Seems so un-natural. So impossible."

"Well as you know, even she was dumbfounded by Tameka. Can you imagine how hard it had to be for her to have to admit that her own child was obviously mentally disturbed? That's a hard pill to swallow."

"I'm sure it is. Did you see how worn Tameka looked? I still can't believe that they let her walk around free like that."

"With so little time left to serve, I guess the officer figured she wouldn't do anything to jeopardize her parole."

"Seeing her today was a shock, but I guess I'd better get used to the idea that I may possibly be seeing her around town very soon. Damned unfair, seven short years and she's free. A murderer walks after just seven lousy years. I don't know if I'm ready to deal with her, Eric."

"I don't expect for you to deal with her. I want you to promise me that you'll treat her just as you did today. If you see her out around the city, ignore her. Keep moving as if she doesn't exist. I don't want her having anything to do with you. Brook, she is poison and has to be kept away. Do you hear me? I mean what I'm saying."

"Eric, you sound like my father instead of my man."

"I just don't trust her. She can never be rehabilitated and I don't want you in harm's way. The best way to ensure that is to pretend like she does not exist. I just want you and the kids safe. Agreed?"

"Agreed, baby. I'll never have anything to do with her again. Tameka Williams is dead to me."

After relaxing in Eric's arms for a while, Brook decided to head up to bed. She was mentally drained and just wanted to sleep. An hour after drifting off, Brook jerked, moaned, and sat straight up in the bed gasping for air. She looked around and realized that she was alone in her bedroom. She ran her hand over her head and brought down a sweaty palm. She got out of bed and splashed a little water on her face. Brook had never had a nightmare before, but damn if Tameka wasn't terrorizing her tonight. Brook began to pray for God to take this haunting away and let her find a restful sleep.

5:00a.m. and Brook was wide awake. She went down to the kitchen to prepare a pot of coffee. It was another two hours before Eric emerged dressed and ready for work. He looked at Brook and could tell that she was out of sorts.

"Are you okay, baby?"

"Sure, I'm fine."

"You don't look like you're fine. What's the matter?"

"Just had a restless night. I'll be fine. As soon as I get my babies back today, I'll be happy and satisfied."

"What time are you going to pick them up?"

"I'm not; Mia is bringing them home at noon. Here is some coffee to go. Have a good day, sweetie."

"I will and if you need me, just call and I'll come running." Eric kissed his wife goodbye and headed out of the house.

Brook went upstairs and began to work. The harder she tried to concentrate on business, the more her thoughts drifted to Ms. Williams. It's as if the realization of her death was just setting in. This really was another great loss for Brook. There was no mother or mother figure in her life, only memories of the women that left her. Of course, there was also the memory of Tameka. Memories of the one person she wished she could erase forever.

The sound of the security buzzer startled Brook and snatched her from her train of thought. When she realized what the noise was, she hopped up and ran to buzz Mia in. Her babies were home and that excited Brook to no end. She stood in the doorway with open arms and of course the kids ran straight to her.

"Hello my babies."

"Hi Mommy," Kristen and Michael sang in unison.

"How are you guys? Did you have fun with Auntie Mia?"

"If you'd let Auntie Mia in we could tell you all about their visit," Mia said with a smirk on her face.

"Oh, be quiet and get in here."

Before Brook could ask them anything else, the children took off to their play room. They had a day off from school and planned to take full advantage of it. Brook and Mia moved to the family room, so that they could get comfortable and talk for a bit.

"Where is Kaylie? I assumed she would be with you. You

know I expect to see my niece each and every time that I see you."

"Well you need to get over that," Mia replied. "Besides, she's riding to the country with her daddy so that she can spend a little time with Grandma Kathy."

"So what are you going to do with the rest of your day?"

"Nothing and I plan to enjoy every second of it. But enough about me, how did things go yesterday?"

"Well, the service was very nice. There were so many people who cared for Ms. Williams. She was very well thought of. And before you ask, yes, Tameka was there. She wasn't hand cuffed or anything and when she entered, she did so on Wayne's arm."

"But she's still a prisoner. They let her go to the service alone?"

"No, there was an officer in the back of the church, and she was driven to the cemetery in a police car. I guess the officer figured that she wouldn't try to escape since she has so little time left to serve."

"I don't care if she only had two hours left to serve, her crazy behind should have
been shackled. Did she attempt to make eye contact with you?"

"Girl, that heffa not only made eye contact; she had the nerve to speak to me."

"I know you are lying."

"Mia, she stood in my face and thanked me for the service for her mom. As if I did all of that for her. I did that service because it's what Ms. Williams deserved."

"Well, did you speak back to her?"

"No! Eric told her that it was what her mom deserved and then we walked away. Mia, I just don't know that I'm ready to have to deal with the fact that that crazy ass woman is going to be free and that we may actually cross paths. The feelings of security and peace I had are being ripped from me."

"Now you can't let her steal your peace. That is something

that God gives you from within. No one should be able to take that from you."

"I know, you're right, but I can't help but feel a little vulnerable. I can't help but think about what she may do once she's released. I'm even having nightmares about this idiot."

"What kind of nightmares?" Mia asked with great concern.

"Last night I dreamt that she was holding a pillow over Kristen's face while screaming that I had ruined her life. I honestly woke up in a cold sweat."

"Did you share this with Eric?"

"No, he's already advising me to pretend that she doesn't even exist and to completely ignore her if I were to ever see her around town. That may be easier said than done."

"Why, Brook? I would think that it would be easy to ignore her. She has no place in your life anymore."

"I know you guys are right. I just have to stop thinking about her. With Ms. Williams gone, we have nothing that could ever tie us together or cause us to be in one another's presence. I'm letting it go and forgetting about that girl."

# CHAPTER SEVEN

Tameka was sitting at a table in the common area thinking about her mom and her loss. Her work detail had been suspended, providing her with more free time to think about her situation and that wasn't necessarily a good thing. She was actually feeling a little hopeless. Since her mother's funeral, her brother had packed up and moved to Arizona, partly to get a fresh start with a new career and partly to escape the law. He had had enough of dealing drugs and recently he'd barely escaped a police trap. He and everyone else knew that the cops were out to get him.

It was true that she still had Wayne. He had been with her through this whole ordeal, but realistically, how long would he continue to be by her side? For all Tameka knew, he could have a new love and just hadn't told her in an effort to keep her positive while she was doing her time.

"Are you ready for your therapy session, Tameka?" Officer Todd asked as he approached her table.

"Do I have a choice?"

"We always have choices," he replied.

"Okay, no sermons today; let's just go."

Without any further conversation, Officer Todd escorted

Tameka through the halls of hell to her therapy session. Once there, he opened the door to allow Tameka entrance and then locked the door as he made his departure. Tameka casually took a seat on the chaise.

"How are you today, Tameka?" Dr. Lamb inquired.

"I'm here."

"Is that all, just here?"

"That's what I said, isn't it?"

"Wow, who pissed in your cornflakes this morning?"

"No one, I just can't think of a reason to be very happy right now. I've got no reason to be cheerful."

"Tameka, did you forget that you go before the parole board in five days? Honey, for all intensive purposes, you are out of here in five days. That's something to be jumping for joy about."

"And where will I go Dr. Lamb? Who will I have when I leave? My mother up and died on me and my brother left town before I even had a chance to go before the board. So please, remind me again what I have to be so damn happy about."

"Tameka, you still have Wayne. He has been your rock, remember. Wayne has remained a constant in your life. His faith in you and his loyalty to you have never wavered. That is huge! Most of these women in here have never known real love, but you've had it all along. Wayne has loved you through all of this. That is something to be happy about."

"Yeah, Doc, but how long will it take for me to become invisible to him just as I've become invisible to everyone else outside of these walls?"

"What makes you think you're invisible to everyone outside of this prison?"

"Remember when you asked me if I saw Brook at my mom's funeral and I said no?"

"Yes, I remember."

"Well, I lied, I did see her and her husband Eric. They both looked like a million bucks. Life, as usual, has been good to Brook. I even attempted to speak to her. I simply wanted to thank her for the service she put together for my mom. Do you know what her response was?"

"No, Tameka, tell me."

"Nothing… She looked right through me. It was as if I were a ghost, something you think you might have seen but not significant enough to warrant a second glance. That bitch wouldn't even acknowledge my words."

"Really Tameka, did you honestly expect anything more from her? I'm sure she is still very hurt by your actions. Losing a child is a very painful experience, but to lose a child at the hands of a supposed friend, that's down right traumatic. Quite honestly, you should never expect anything more than hatred from Brook."

"Let me understand this, you are my therapist, but you're taking her side?"

"Tameka, I'm on the side of truth and honesty. I'm just trying to clearly lay out the facts for you so that you don't have unrealistic expectations. You kill a woman's baby you shouldn't expect her to be your friend."

Tameka's anger forced her from her seat and sent her stomping back and forth across the floor. Her jaw was tight, eye's narrow, and breath heavy. Dr. Lamb could almost see the smoke escaping from her nostrils.

"Tameka, I understand that the truth is sometimes a painful thing, but it has to be
    accepted."

"So I have to accept that she gets to move on with her life and be happy while I have to try and start life all over again. Everyone seems to forget that I lost a baby too. What makes her child's life any more valuable than mine?"

"No one said that her baby's life was more valuable than your baby's life. However, your baby's death was due to a miscarriage that was not caused by another person; it was the result of an accident, an unfortunate fall. Brook lost her child because you secretly fed her drugs. Can you honestly tell me that you don't see the difference?"

"That's not the point, damn it!"

"Tameka, I need for you to calm down…now! Take your seat, or I'll have to end this session."

Tameka stomped and huffed over to her seat as if she were a child. She laid back on the seat in an effort to calm her nerves. While Tameka took several deep breaths, Dr. Lamb retrieved her a glass of water.

"You don't have anything stronger than this?" Tameka asked in a joking manner.

"You wish."

Dr. Lamb returned to her seat and quietly contemplated if Tameka was really ready for this release. Was she really as rehabilitated as she claimed to be? Was Tameka truly ready to be released into society? More importantly, was society ready for Tameka?

# CHAPTER EIGHT

Tameka sat nervously in a small room with her attorney waiting for the parole board's decision. She didn't see how they could possibly turn her down. There was no one from her victim's family to speak out against her, but Dr. Lamb and Wayne both spoke on her behalf. She just wished that they would hurry up. The suspense of it all was killing her. Patients had never been Tameka's strong suit, so this waiting around for such a life changing decision was maddening for her.

"How much longer do you think it will be?" Tameka asked the short, fat, balding man that Wayne had hired to serve as her legal council.

"Tameka, we've only been waiting five minutes. Sit back and relax; they will let us know what they've decided shortly."

"Relax my ass; if I get turned down you still get to go home tonight. I'll be the one stuck here. Do you think they are going to make me serve more time?"

"Tameka, we had good witnesses and presented a good case for release, that's all I can say. I can't predict what they will actually do. As hard as it is, you'll have to be patient."

It was clear from the attorney's tone that he was becoming impatient with Tameka. He was aware of what was at stake for her but Tameka had to know that he wasn't a fortune teller. He really needed for her to sit still and hush before he lost his temper.

A frail, middle aged man stepped out into the hall and advised that a decision had been reached. He held the door while Tameka, her attorney, Wayne, and Dr. Lamb all filed back in. Wayne sat directly behind Tameka and lovingly rubbed her back as they waited for the decision to be rendered. A young, very robust, red headed woman looked at Tameka and began to speak.

"Ms. Williams, we have carefully looked over your file, your prison history, and taken into account all that the witnesses had to say on your behalf. We have decided at this time to grant your release with the following conditions: You will remain on probation for the next five years. You must attend anger management classes weekly as well as perform one hundred fifty hours of community service over the course of one year. If you fail to report to your parole officer, fail to attend the classes or complete your community service, you will be thrown back in prison to serve the remainder of your sentence. If you even think about stepping outside of the boundaries of the law, you will be returned to this prison. Do you understand?"

"Yes ma'am and thank you all so much. I promise you won't be sorry."

"You just make sure that we are not. Goodbye and good luck, Ms. Williams."

Tameka spun around and was swept up into a bear hug by Wayne. He held her while she cried tears of joy. Finally, she could start her life over again. Her only regret was that her mom was not here to see it. Once Wayne released her from their embrace, Dr. Lamb congratulated her with a hug of her own.

"Thank you for everything, Dr. Lamb. There's no way I would have been released without your testimony."

"You are very welcome, Tameka. Now I want you to go out there and make me proud. And I want you to promise me that you'll contact that therapist that I referred you to. She'll be expecting your call. I promise you'll love her."

"I will, Dr. Lamb. Wayne here will make sure of that."

"You got that right," chimed Wayne.

Tameka turned to her attorney, "So what's next?"

"Well, I'll get the paperwork filed today, and it usually takes twenty-four to forty-eight hours for everything to go through. Then you'll be free as a bird."

Tameka thanked and hugged everyone once more before being escorted back to her block. She had been so careful not to let herself get excited by the possibility of freedom, but now that it was actually happening, she was overjoyed. Her mind was flying with all of the things that she wanted and needed to do, she didn't know where to begin. How do you start life again after seven long years of someone else telling you what to do?

"Penny for your thoughts?" asked Officer Todd.

"Man, my head is spinning. I'm so excited about getting out of here but kind of scared about how things will be going forward. Trying to figure out how to start over is mind blowing."

"My advice would be to start with God. This is a great opportunity for you to pray for direction. Immerse yourself in His word and find a good church home. If you consult God and put Him first, He will lead you in the right direction."

"I hear you, Todd. I promise to take that under advisement."

Two days later, Tameka found herself dressed in the clothes that Wayne had brought her and packing up the few personal items that she had. Officer Todd was waiting to escort her out of the building and through the gates to her freedom. As Tameka started her walk out of the block, her fellow inmates began to applaud. She could hear words of encouragement mixed with some snide comments warning her that she'd be back.

At the last stop, she was presented with $587.65, her earnings from the work she'd done over the past seven years. The other items that were confiscated when she first arrived were now returned. She took her belongings and made her exit.

# CHAPTER NINE

"So, what would you like to do first, baby? The world is now your oyster, whatever you want, we can make it happen."

"Wayne, nothing would make me happier than to go home and soak in a steaming hot bath. I want to get the stench of that ungodly place off of me. Then, baby, I want a real meal."

"What do you have a taste for?"

"How about some Italian? I have had dreams about that Chicken Marsala."

"Then Carrabba's it is."

"Oh, you know what? I don't have any clothes. All that stuff I left at Brooks is either out dated or I'm sure, too small."

"Well, I was very confident that you would get paroled, so I went on a mini shopping spree for you. I bought you enough things to tide you over until you feel up to going shopping for yourself."

"You are the best, Wayne. I can't thank you enough for standing by me through all of this. Most people with the best of intentions would have moved on with someone else after about a year. For you to wait on me for seven years is simply unbelievable. It speaks so much to your character and is a testament to kind of man that you are. Thank you."

Tameka reached over and took Wayne's free hand in hers. She held onto him tightly as they drove through the city streets. Tameka looked around in amazement. It was as if she were visiting Atlanta for the first time. She could not believe the changes that had taken place since she was last free to explore her own city. Atlanta had always been a wonderful city, but it was now extraordinary. The growth was amazing. All of the multi-function communities seemed to fascinate Tameka.

Wayne maneuvered his car through his sub-division and finally pulled into the garage. Tameka was so relieved to be at the house. It symbolized for her that the freedom she'd been granted was real. She was home; there would be no return trip to prison. She was indeed home.

As soon as Tameka hit the door, she began to peel off her clothes. She went directly to the bath room and began to draw a hot bubble bath. While the water ran and steamed up the room, she lit candles and selected some soothing music to listen to while she soaked. Once the tub was full, Tameka eased into the water and allowed it to melt away all of her anxiety. This was the greatest moment she'd experienced in the past seven years.

An hour and a half later, Tameka emerged from the bedroom dressed and ready to go. Wayne stepped to her, pulled her into his arms and kissed her passionately.

"You look beautiful, baby."

"I have to say, Wayne, I feel like a new woman. I'm ready for a new life, ready for a fresh start."

"Well for now we'll start with dinner. Ready to go?"

"Yes, let's go eat" Tameka sang as she grabbed Wayne's hand.

The restaurant was quite busy, but fortunately they were seated right away. After placing their drink order, Tameka excused herself for the restroom. Tameka washed her hands, checked herself in the mirror, and walked out. As she made her way back to the table, she noticed that someone else had stopped and was talking to Wayne. He was a tall, handsome man that looked vaguely familiar. Tameka stopped and watched the exchange between the two men. They interacted as if they were old friends. A few seconds later, the man shook Wayne's hand and placed the other hand on the back of Wayne's neck. He said his goodbyes and walked away. When he approached the front door, he took the hand of a woman standing with a little girl. The woman took one more glance over her shoulder, and that's when Tameka and Mia's eyes locked. After a second or two, Mia swooped up her daughter and walked out of the door.

"Who was that man?" Tameka demanded as she approached the table.

"David, why?"

"He was the guy dating Mia when I left. You remember Mia, Brook's best friend."

"Yeah, I remember her, but she and David are married now. Have been for a few years."

"I never realized that you even knew David. When did you two become buddies and why didn't you tell me you'd been hanging out with my enemies, Wayne?"

"Baby, I'm not hanging out with your enemies. I met David through work, and I've never hung out with him and his wife. I've never even told him that I know who his wife is. None of that past stuff has ever come up."

"That's hard to believe after witnessing how chummy you two were. You all acted as if you grew up together or something. You know, like childhood friends."

"It's not even like that Tameka. Just doing what I have to in order to maintain a good business relationship."

"Yeah, whatever."

# CHAPTER TEN

David and Mia had been riding in silence since leaving the restaurant. David could sense that something was wrong but didn't care enough to ask what the problem was. It seemed that all he and Mia did lately was argue so the quiet ride home was fine with him.

"When the hell did you become friends with Tameka's boyfriend?"

"Who?"

"The guy you were skinning and grinning with in the restaurant, that was Wayne. I didn't realize it until I locked eyes with Tameka. You remember Tameka, the crazy murderer that caused Brook to lose her first child. Please, baby, please tell me when you decided you needed him as friend?" Mia screeched through clinched teeth.

"Mia, I'm sorry, I didn't realize that he had any connection to Tameka. I mean he's just a dude I met though a mutual friend. He seemed like a cool brotha so we started going out for a beer every now and then. He never mentioned anything about Tameka. I swear."

"This all seems very strange to me, David. You have plenty of friends already. Why would you start hanging out with Wayne? I mean does Eric ever hang out with ya'll as well?"

"Baby, you know that Eric is always up under Brook. He seems to only have time for his precious wife and kids. No time to hang out with the fellas. Brook had his nose wide open from jump, and she's had him whipped ever since." David chuckled.

"So Eric's devotion to his family is amusing to you? Wow, we've become so different. Family, love, and devotion was something that we both used to think were the most important things in the world. Now, you find them funny. You think that loving your wife and child makes you whipped."

"That's not what I meant."

"But that's what you said."

"Mia, maybe if you weren't always bitching, I wouldn't find the thought of spending every waking moment with you funny...or nauseating." David spat at his wife.

Mia turned her head to look out the window so that David couldn't see the tears streaming down her face. She couldn't figure out what had gone so terribly wrong between them. His undying love for her had turned into seething hatred somewhere along the way. Mia was growing weary from the constant arguing and lack of affection. She didn't know how much longer she could take it. As soon as David pulled into the garage, Mia got out of the car, picked up their sleeping princess from the back seat, and walked into the house. She wasn't at all surprised to hear David back the car right back out of the garage and take off down the street.

Mia dropped Kaylie off at pre-k and returned home to finish cleaning and preparing brunch for her and Book. After David crept in the house around 2:30 am and was gone for work by 6:00 am, Mia decided to call Brook and ask her to come over. She wanted to tell Brook about seeing Tameka, but she also felt that she needed to vent about her personal life. She needed her friend now more than ever. Mia felt that she needed a shoulder to cry on as well as someone to understand her point of view regarding all of the marital issues that she and David were having. It wasn't long before she heard the doorbell ring.

"Good morning, Brook. How are you today?" Mia asked as she stepped to the side to allow Brook entry into her beautifully decorated middle-class home.

"Hey, Mia, I'm good. How about you? I have to say, you didn't sound so great on the phone earlier."

"I'm okay; just have a lot on my mind. But we'll get to all of that. For now, come on in and join me for brunch. I'm starving."

"Me too, girl. Whatever you've prepared smells delicious."

"How do you feel about an omelet? I have ham, cheese, mushrooms, onions, peppers and tomatoes all prepped. You just tell me what you want in yours and it won't take but a second to cook."

"Now that sounds delicious. I'll have ham, cheese and onion in mine. And I think I'll pour myself a cup of coffee while you do the omelets."

"Knock yourself out."

Brook added sugar and cream to her coffee and took a seat at the bar. She watched as Mia cooked their food. She couldn't help but notice how melancholy Mia seemed. Couldn't help but notice the worry lines that seemed to have settled into her friend's forehead. Brook's concern for Mia was growing by the minute. What could have Mia so out of sorts?

Mia sat their plates down on the bar and filled a couple of glasses with cranberry juice. She took a seat opposite of Brook and held her hand out for her friend to hold as they prayed over their meal.

"Umm, this is so good. It's been a long time since I've had a good omelet."

"Well, I'm glad you like it. Nice to know that someone appreciates my cooking."

"Mia, what's wrong? What's going on with you? You don't seem like yourself at all."

"How about we finish our meal and then talk?"

"Whatever you say."

They ate and drank in silence for the next ten minutes or so. Once Brook was finished, she got up and took her dishes to the sink. She grabbed the plastic lids from the counter and began to place them on the bowls containing the various ingredients used in the omelets. She placed the covered bowls in the refrigerator and turned around only to notice Mia weeping. Brook walked over and took Mia in her arms. As she embraced her friend, Mia's silent weeping changed to all out crying. She balled as if she were a sixteen year old that had just suffered her first broken heart. After purging her soul of its apparent grief, Brook took her by the hand and led her to the sofa in the family room.

"Mia, what in the world is going on? What can I do to help?"

"There's nothing to be done. I'm pretty sure that my marriage is over."

"Now Mia, I know that you and David have been having some difficulties, but don't you think its way too soon to be talking divorce?"

"You don't understand, Brook, we can't talk to one another without it turning into an argument. I mean we barely even say 'hi' and 'bye' to each other any more. And I can't even tell you the last time we made love. Oh wait a minute, that's a lie. We made love or should I say had sex, five weeks ago. Brook, he makes it seem as if it is such an imposition to be with me. I don't even want him to touch me anymore. The last time, he man handled me as if I were some hooker off the street. I swear I don't know who he is anymore. I feel like I'm living with a stranger."

"When did you first start to notice the changes in David's behavior?"

"Well, you know that things became really strained with us

after Brady passed, but the arrival of Kaylie seemed to have breathed new life into our marriage. But, Brook, things began to take a turn for the worse, the weird, and the odd about a year ago."

Brady, Mia and David's first child, was a beautiful, full term baby. But blood tests revealed that he had Sickle Cell Disease. Mia nor David thought to do any genetic testing prior to getting pregnant. They both carried the Sickle Cell trait and their child paid the price. As the months went on, Brady's belly became abnormally enlarged. Blood was beginning to gather in his spleen, an unfortunate but common symptom for infants with Sickle Cell. This was the cause of Brady's death when he was just an innocent nine-month-old baby. After his death, instead of Mia and David turning to one another, they turned on each other. They played the blame game and each of them cried alone. Finally, they sought counseling and were able to work through their pain together. One could only imagine their relief when Kaylie was born with just the trait and not the disease.

"I hate to ask, but do you think David's having an affair?"

"If he is, it must be with a hell of a woman because she has turned him out. I mean his behavior in the bedroom is totally different. His attitude towards me is nothing like it used to be. He has only been consistently kind to Kaylie. When he is in her presence, he is the sweetest man. But when she is asleep or away from home, it's like I'm living with the devil."

"Have you all considered counseling again? It really helped you guys deal with the loss of Brady."

"I've suggested it, but he has no interest in counseling at all. Let's face it Brook, his interests now lie outside of this house. I don't know what they are and I don't have a clue as to how to get him interested in me again. Frankly, I don't know if I want him to be interested anymore."

"You don't mean that. You love David."

"Like Tina said, `what's love got to do with it?' Lord knows I don't want anyone that doesn't want me back. And on that note, I've made a decision."

"And what would that be?"

"I'm going to file for legal separation."

"Mia, you don't mean that. You're just upset."

"No, no. I was upset, but now I'm seeing things very clearly. This is what I need to do." Mia stated very matter-of-factly. "Now moving on, you'll never guess who I saw yesterday."

"Who?

"Tameka Williams."

"What the hell? Where did you see her?"

"Carrabba's. We went there for dinner and I was standing at the front door waiting as David spoke with some guy he knows. Turns out that the guy was Wayne. I realized this when Tameka emerged from the restroom to take her place at the table with her man."

"Well, evil dwells among us once again."

# CHAPTER ELEVEN

Tameka stood outside of the television station and took a couple of deep breaths before walking through the glass door. She was trying her best not to let her nerves get the best of her. Tameka's parole officer had given her several job leads but this was the one she really wanted. This position would put her back in the television news arena that she so desperately wanted to regain entry into. It, of course, wasn't a station as big as CNN, where she once worked; it was just a small local cable station. And naturally she wouldn't be the TV personality she once was, but this entry level position was a foot in the door. Tameka slowly approached the receptionist.

"Good morning, my name is Tameka Williams. I have a 10:00 appointment with Mrs. Gillman."

"Yes Ms. Williams, she's expecting you. Please follow me."

Tameka followed the scrawny little woman down a narrow hall to a small room full of cubicles. At the back of the room was a small, glass enclosed office. The receptionist tapped on the office door, gently opened it and announced Tameka's arrival.

"Please, come in," Mrs. Gillman welcomed Tameka with an extended hand. Tameka shook the woman's hand and took a seat opposite Mrs. Gillman's desk. As she waited for Mrs. Gillman to finish shuffling through some papers, Tameka took a couple of more deep breaths and said yet another silent prayer.

"So Ms. Williams, why don't you tell me a little bit about yourself?"

"I am a graduate of Spellman College. I worked for CNN a total of two years. The first year and a half I worked as a producer and the last six months I was the lead noon day anchor."

"Well that type of experience could certainly come in handy around here. However, I see that you haven't worked for the past seven years. Would you mind telling me about how that time was spent?"

Tameka nervously looked about the office as she rang her hands together. This was the question she had hoped to avoid. "Well, um Mrs. Gillman, I...I"

"Please Ms. Williams, talk to me honestly."

"I was in state prison, Mrs. Gillman." Tameka flatly replied.

"Of course I knew that, but I would like to hear about your situation from you as opposed to reading this form letter from your parole officer."

Tameka inhaled and started talking. "I was on a date with a young man when we decided to go back to his place for a night cap. Once there, he began to make very forceful advances. I pleaded with him to stop, but he kept on assaulting me. As a means of protecting myself, I grabbed a beer bottle and hit him with it. This angered him, and he hit me. I felt I had no choice but to hit him again with the broken bottle. Unfortunately, the broken glass cut a major artery, and he died. I pled guilty to manslaughter and served seven years."

"So you took responsibility for your actions. That's good. Do you feel that you would now be able to be a productive team member, or do you need more time to adjust to life away from prison?"

"Ma'am, I am completely ready to return to the work force. I want the opportunity to work my way up from the bottom, to show you what I am capable of. I know that I would be an asset to your team. Please just give me the chance."

"Ms. Williams, you have a ninety day trial period. Don't give me a reason to show you the door. This small station has been a great stepping stone for many news reporters, and it could be the same for you. Don't screw it up."

"I won't, Mrs. Gillman. Thank you so much. I will not make you regret this decision to give me chance."

Tameka literally danced back to her car. She finally had something to be excited about, something to look forward to. She thought that she'd never get the opportunity to work in the news field again, but God had shown her mercy, had given her a second chance. She swore that she wouldn't screw it up this time.

By the time Wayne made it home, Tameka had finished preparing a fabulous celebratory dinner. Wayne walked into the kitchen, sniffing as if he were some type of hound dog.

"What is that wonderful aroma?"

"That would be smothered chicken, rice pilaf and asparagus. I hope you're hungry."

"I'm starved. I was so busy today that I skipped lunch. My tank is definitely running on empty. But I have to say, I'm surprised you cooked."

"What do you mean? I'm a good cook."

"I know that, but I assumed you were trying to eat out every day to celebrate your freedom."

"Well I decided to cook to celebrate my employment."

"You got that entry position at the station?"

"Yep."

"Baby, that's great. I'm very happy for you. When do you start?"

"I start first thing Monday morning. That gives me only five days to get a decent wardrobe together. I don't want to start my new job looking like some throw away child. So, baby, are you going to sponsor my little shopping spree? I promise it will be the last time. Soon I'll have my own cash and won't need to pester you."

"You are not pestering me, and of course I'll sponsor your shopping spree. Well, I'll sponsor $2500.00 worth of shopping. After that, you're on your own."

"Thank you, Wayne. You are my angel."

Tameka spent the weekend running from one store to the other. She was determined to stretch that $2500.00 until it cried for mercy. This was definitely a time for bargain hunting. The trips to Phipps Plaza would have to wait until she was earning her own money...big money. But just for old time sake, she did duck into the MAC store at Perimeter Mall. Tameka would not go cheap on her make up. Her face had to be flawless. She paid for her purchases and turned to leave the store. As soon as she spun around, she was face-to-face with Brook. Knowing that her greeting would be ignored, Tameka chose to drop her head and rush out the door. A few feet from the entrance to the store, Tameka stopped cold and thought "Hell I've paid my debt to society. That heffa will not run me out of anywhere." Tameka then returned to the store.

"Hello Brook. It's good to see you, how have you been?"

Brook took her receipt from the sales lady, moved around Tameka and kept stepping as if she didn't hear a word from Tameka's mouth. Tameka was embarrassed and angry. She decided to follow Brook from the store.

"Brook, I know you heard me. Don't ignore me as if I don't exist." Continuing to follow Brook, Tameka shouted "Answer me damn it!"

Brook spun around, looked Tameka in the eye with an unmistakable hatred. "I will warn you only once, leave me alone.

Never speak to me again or I will go take out a restraining order and press charges for harassment. So unless you want to go back to prison, heed my warning and stay the hell away from me."

Tameka was left standing in the middle of the mall looking stupid and feeling like less than zero.

# CHAPTER TWELVE

Brook returned home to her family after her brief shopping trip. She prepared dinner, bathed her kids and put them to bed. She was looking forward to spending the rest of the evening with Eric. She was still fuming over her run in with Tameka and knew that her man would calm her nerves and put her mind at ease. Brook poured a couple of glasses of wine and joined Eric in the family room.

"Alright, baby, what's got you so annoyed?"

"How do you know I'm annoyed?"

"You're my wife; I know everything about you and can read you like a book. So speak up woman, what's bothering you."

"One guess as to whom I ran into today. Go ahead, take a guess."

"Come on now, you know I hate all that guessing crap, just tell me."

"Tameka Williams! And that woman had the nerve to follow me out of the store. She was determined to make me speak to her. Like we were going to re-new that warped friendship we once had. I swear she's just as crazy as she ever was."

"Well what did you say to her? Did you respond in any way

because I thought we agreed that you would ignore her at all costs?"

"Well I was ignoring her until she called me out in the middle of the mall. Then I advised her that if she ever approached or spoke to me again that I would take out a restraining order and send her right back to prison."

"And how did she react to that?"

"I don't know. I walked off and left her ass in the middle of the mall."

"I hate to say it baby but we knew that this was bound to happen. You all used to travel in the same circles and you knew that she'd try to resume her old life style. As big as Atlanta is, you two will occasionally run into each other. And as much as I wish I could kill her for all she's done, we're going to just have to accept that seeing her is something that is going to happen."

"But it's not fair. She still belongs behind bars."

"I agree but there is nothing we can do about that. The law says she's paid her debt to society. But it sounds like you handled the situation very well. I like it when you put your foot down." Eric moaned as he kissed Brook on the neck.

"Stop trying to distract me."

Eric ignored Brook's last comment and continued to nibble at her neck. She giggled which let him know that she'd relaxed her mood and was open to his advances. Eric moved from her neck to her lips. He gently caressed her face and moved further down her body. Her husband became more aggressive, and Brook could feel herself melting. As Eric took his wife right there on the floor, she went from a state of anger to one of euphoria.

While Brook was having her nerves soothed by her husband, Tameka had fallen into a black hole of anger. Despite everything she'd done to Brook, she still didn't feel that Brook's reaction to her was justified. As far as Tameka was concerned, it had been seven years and Brook now had two children. It was way past time for Brook to be over all that had happened. It was clear to

Tameka that Brook was the one that hadn't learned any lessons in the past seven years. Brook was the one still living in the bubble of her perfect world, thinking she was still better than everyone else, feeling that the world should bow down before her. She was going to keep on and force Tameka to teach her yet another lesson.

The door slammed closed, yanking Tameka out of trance. She spun around to see Wayne dropping his briefcase on the floor.

"Hey, Wayne."

"Hey, what's going on?" Wayne asked as he walked over and kissed Tameka on the cheek.

"Babe, you'll never believe it. I was out shopping when I bumped into Brook. That bitch didn't even want to acknowledge me and…"

"Stop, okay, just stop."

"What the hell is wrong with you?"

"I've had a long, hard day and the last damn thing I want to hear about is some mess with you and Brook. Pretend like you don't know her and leave her the hell alone and you shouldn't have any problems and I won't ever have to hear anything about the two of you again."

Wayne moved passed Tameka and made his way to the bedroom. Tameka was stunned and couldn't move for a minute. Wayne had never spoken to her like this before. Despite everything she'd done, the hard years that had passed, he'd never raised his voice to her in that manner.

After absorbing what had just happened, Tameka decided to join Wayne in the bedroom and try to smooth things over. She found him in the shower and figured what the hell. This will be the perfect way to apologize. Tameka stripped down and joined Wayne in the shower. She soaped her hands and began to rub him down.

"I'm sorry, baby. I didn't mean to dump on you as soon as you got in the door. It won't happen again."

"I don't mind you telling me about your day or your troubles, as long as none of it includes Brook Mansfield-Banks. You should be so far beyond all of this by now. Let it go."

"You're right and I will. I'll let it all go." Tameka purred as she began to kiss Wayne passionately. He returned the kiss but to Tameka's surprise, he became more forceful than he'd ever been. He kissed and caressed her and without warning, spun her around and pinned her against the wall. He took her right there as the water beat down on them. It was completely mind blowing, and Tameka reached her peak in record time. Suddenly, Wayne cut the water off and led Tameka to the bed, laid her on her stomach and took her again but in a way he never had before. This was the first time Tameka had ever experienced anal sex and it was all a little too forceful for her. But Wayne seemed to have enjoyed it more than he'd ever enjoyed anything they had done in the past. In no time, he reached orgasm and collapsed on her back.

Tameka spoke slowly with a shaky voice. "What the hell was that?"

"Just wanted to try something new, and it was *great*. We should do it like this more often, huh?"

Tameka just laid there feeling numb. "Are you okay, baby?" Wayne asked."

"Don't you think we should've talked about that first, you know, make sure it was cool with me?"

"I'm sorry; I thought you'd enjoy a spur of the moment change up. Didn't you like it?"

Tameka didn't answer. Instead her mind was flying, wondering when her man had gotten a taste of this and who was he with when he discovered it.

# CHAPTER THIRTEEN

It was Friday night and Brook had convinced Mia to go out with her. Brook thought a girl's night out might cheer Mia up a little. Unfortunately, things hadn't gotten any better between Mia and David. The sad part was that despite how beautiful and brilliant Mia was, she was starting to blame herself for all of their problems and feel as if all of this was happening because she was no longer attractive enough to hold her husband's interest.

"Alright Mr. Mom, I'm going to head out now. Are you sure you're going to be okay with the kids?"

"Of course I am. We're going to eat pizza and ice cream and watch movies, aren't we guys?"

The kids screamed "yes" in unison, unable to contain their excitement.

"Well okay, but don't eat too much or stay up too late."

"Yes, Mommy," Eric sang with a smirk on his face.

"Funny. I shouldn't be too late." Brook kissed Eric and moved on to her children.

"Goodnight ya'll. Be good and keep an eye on Daddy." Brook kissed them goodbye and left.

Brook drove through the city, still captivated by the beauty of the Atlanta skyline. She had never, for one moment, regretted making Atlanta her home. Of course there were things about Baltimore that she missed, but with her parents gone, she was no longer comfortable there. She went back to visit her extended family a few times each year, but the trips were always short. She only stayed long enough to say hello and make sure that her most elder family members were okay and being properly taken care of. She knew that her mom would want her to at least do that.

Brook pulled into Mia's driveway, took a deep breath, and made her way to the front door. She hoped with all her might that Mia would enjoy herself and use this outing as a way to relieve some stress. Before Brook could ring the doorbell, Mia swung the door open to greet her friend.

"Hey girl, come on in. I just have to get my shoes on and I'll be ready." Brook stepped into the house, closing the door behind her. She looked around and even stepped into the hall looking around as if she'd misplaced something.

"Where is Kaylie?"

"She's sleeping over at her best friend's house. According to her friend's mom, they are going to have a princess party. So you know I'll get an ear full from Kaylie tomorrow."

"Oh, you can bet on that. But I am a little disappointed."

"Why?"

"I assumed she'd be here with David and I'd have a few minutes to spend with her."

"David spends as little time as possible here now. I'm starting to wonder if he has another home somewhere."

"Well the hell with him, at least for tonight."

Mia finished putting the final touches on her makeup and stepped into her shoes. "I'm ready." She sang as she entered the room.

"Damn, girl, you look good."

"Thanks, now let's roll."

It didn't take long for the Lucky Lounge to get filled to capacity. Fortunately, they arrived early enough to snag a table.

They soaked up the atmosphere. It was a great change of pace for them both. Brook was surprised by how much she actually enjoyed being out without the family. This was a serious reminder for her that she needed to tend to herself as much as she did her family. The girl's night out would have to happen more often. They sipped their wine and engaged in light conversation while Jamie Foxx played in the background, encouraging them to blame bad behavior on the alcohol.

"So Eric didn't have an issue with you hanging out tonight did he?"

"Girl, get real. You know Eric doesn't care. He thinks we should make this a monthly thing. Says that we need to blow off some steam every now and then."

"Um, he may be on to something."

"You got that right, we deserve a break from the mommy and wifey mode. Especially you Mia. You're almost like a single parent now."

"I don't even want to think or talk about that tonight. I just want to enjoy myself, and I can't do that thinking about David's trifling behind."

"I'm sorry."

"No worries. You have nothing to apologize… "

Before Mia could finish her sentence, the server returned to the table with their food order. Neither Brook nor Mia wasted any time digging in. They ate, drank, laughed, and talked and Mia seemed to escape all of her worries, if only for a while anyway. As the evening went on, Mia came to realize that she still had what it took to attract a man, even if the man wasn't her husband. She was reminded by several men just how beautiful she was. Mia was turning them away left and right, but it was clear that she was flattered by all of the attention. There was one guy in particular who was indeed a fine specimen of a man. He bought the ladies a round of drinks and passed Mia his business card. She accepted the card just to be polite, and when he walked away, she eased it right on into her purse.

The night had been perfect, until Mia spotted her husband walk in and make his way over to the far end of the bar. Brook followed Mia's gaze, and they watched as David ordered his drink and turn to survey his surroundings. Fortunately, he didn't spot them. He moved around the bar to where a couple of ladies were standing. He seemed to know them already. He ordered drinks for them and once the cocktails were placed on the bar, he slid one to one of the girls but picked the other up, placed it in the other chicks hand as he leaned in and kissed her neck.

"What the hell?" was all Mia could seem to let escape her mouth.

"Come on Mia, let's just go. It's pretty late anyway."

"We'll leave in a minute."

David talked to the ladies a few moments more until another man walked up and smacked him on the shoulder. David turned and greeted the guy with a brother man hug.

"Oh hell, that's Wayne."

"You mean Tameka's Wayne?" Brook quizzed.

"The one and only, and I can't figure out for the life of me when they had an opportunity to become so damn chummy."

"You know I don't have a clue."

Mia continued to watch as David and Wayne took their drinks and moved to the backside of the room."

"I wonder what they are up to. What do they even have in common that pulls them together as friends?"

"No idea Mia, I have no idea at all. Are you going to let David know that you're here?"

"Hell no, let's go." Mia huffed as she grabbed her purse.

## CHAPTER FOURTEEN

Tameka had finished her first week of employment. She was proud of her new position and had a really good feeling about her co-workers. No one seemed to have been put off by her past. There were no judgments being thrown around. She didn't expect to be well received at all, but was grateful for the warm welcome into the organization. She had been allowed to cut out an hour early so that she could make her first court appointed counseling session on time. Tameka hoped that this new therapist would be okay, but she didn't expect that she'd be able to build the relationship with this one the way she had with Dr. Lamb.

Tameka entered the therapist's office, signed in and began to fill out the paperwork she'd been handed by the receptionist. The questions seemed to go on forever. Tameka was surprised they didn't ask what color her panties were because they sure had asked everything else about her. When she finally finished the forms, she returned them to the receptionist and began to flip through a magazine as she impatiently waited for her session to begin.

"Ms. Williams, I'm ready for you. Please follow me."

Tameka did as she was told and followed the tall, slim, but shapeless therapist back to her office.

"Please, have a seat," The therapist gestured towards the couch.

Again, Tameka obeyed and sat down. She looked around the tastefully decorated office as she waited for the therapist to also take a seat.

"Ms. Williams, allow me to formally introduce myself. I am Constance Weber, but you can call me Connie. We will be working together for the next year or so. I prefer if we keep our sessions relaxed, you know, comfortable for both of us. And of course, anything goes; there is no topic that is off limits."

"I thought that we were only going to be dealing with all the crap having to do with my incarceration?"

"That will of course be part of our sessions, Ms. Williams, but I like to cover everything. You will be surprised at what will come out of our meetings and how much of it had a direct impact on the decision you made that sent you to prison."

"Humph, you talk a lot, don't you Connie?"

"Well, I'll shut up and let you do the talking."

"And what do you want me to talk about, Ms. Connie?"

"Whatever is on your mind."

"Connie, I really don't mean any disrespect, but I have a lot on my mind. So, as the licensed therapist, why don't you suggest a starting point?"

"Fine, I guess I can do that. Why don't you tell me how you plan to handle your first encounter with Brook Mansfield-Banks? That was an issue that seemed to cause Dr. Lamb a great deal of concern."

"That encounter has already happened. We were both in the cosmetics store; she turned around, looked right through me and kept stepping."

"How did that make you feel?"

"It pissed me off. Wouldn't it piss you off to be treated as if you didn't exist?"

"You have to take into account you all's history. Surely you can understand why she would be hesitant to greet you with open arms."

"Hesitant I can understand, but when I approached her, she threatened to take out a restraining order on me if I ever spoke to her again. That was totally unnecessary. I've paid my debt to society and it's time for her to get over her damn self."

"Tameka, the debt you paid had nothing to do with the loss of her child. I'm sure she feels that you've never paid for that. Do you still feel the need to communicate with her at this point?"

"No, absolutely not. If she wants nothing to do with me, I can accept that. It's time for me to put Brook behind me and focus on my future."

"Wow it's great to hear you say that. That attitude will definitely help you continue to move in a positive direction. And speaking of your future, how is the new job coming?"

"Connie, I love it. Everyone has been so accepting of me and incredibly helpful. I know that they are all aware of my past, but it doesn't seem to affect how they treat me. All of my co-workers have been very kind and very respectful. I feel great about the position and the opportunities for advancement."

"That is fabulous and I must say that your optimism is very refreshing."

"Well thank you very much, Ms. Connie."

"Now before we wrap this session up, Tameka, tell me how things are going with your personal life."

"Umm…well things are good. Wayne is still treating me very well."

"There was some hesitation. You sure everything is okay?"

"Nothing is off limits, right?"

"Right."

"Okay, I am concerned about one thing. Wayne and I have always had an amazing sexual connection. We're an adventurous couple, tried a lot of different stuff but anal intercourse was never a part of our sex life. He'd never even mentioned it before, showed no interest. But the other night he decided to flip me over and go for it. Didn't discuss it with me, ask me, nothing. He just went for it. Now I'm wondering what the hell is going on. Why all of a sudden does he want anal sex? Don't you think that's a little strange?"

Connie shifted her weight in her chair and removed her glasses as she contemplated her response.

"Tameka, I don't find it strange at all. Anal sex is a very fulfilling part of many couples' sex lives. Should he have discussed it with you prior to the act? Of course he should have. But because of you all's already adventurous sexual encounters, he may have felt that you'd be open to it."

"But where did he even get this desire from, Connie? He never expressed any interest in it before."

"Here's the part you may not want to hear, Tameka. You were gone for seven years. Do you really think that Wayne was celibate the entire seven years?"

"Oh no, I didn't expect him to be."

"Then it was probably something that he tried with someone else while you were away. He obviously enjoyed it and now wants to share the experience with you."

"Humph, I guess I can accept that. He is still with me, loving me, caring for me and honestly, it wasn't that bad. Maybe I'll even get to a point where I really enjoy it."

"Maybe, Tameka, maybe. Well that's our time for this week. The receptionist will schedule you for next week and remember its okay to call me after hours if you have an emergency. It's always better to call me than to do something stupid, okay?"

"Alright Connie, I'll see you next week."

Tameka decided that Connie was right. Some other chick gave Wayne a taste of something good and now she'd make sure that he continued to enjoy it. Tameka was all about pleasing her man.

Tameka stopped by the grocery store on her way home to pick up a few things. She'd decided to cook something special for Wayne. After gathering all of the necessary ingredients, she picked a good bottle of wine and checked out. As she was leaving the downtown area, she spotted an adult toy store and decided to run in. After a brief conversation with the store clerk, Tameka purchased a tube of Anal Ez. It would show Wayne that she was cool with his new form of pleasure and save her from any more discomfort that this freaky stuff could cause.

# CHAPTER FIFTEEN

Mia was up and about quite early. She was trying to get her sleepy little girl ready for early morning church service. She didn't bother waking David, seeing as he'd only arrived home a few hours ago and wasn't showing any interest in church these days.

"Come on, princess, let's go and eat your oatmeal before we put your dress on. We don't want any accidents, do we?"

"No Mommy, my dress is too pretty for oatmeal."

"Yes it is, baby."

"Mommy, is daddy coming with us to church? He is going to make us late. He knows that you get mad when we're late."

"Well, Kaylie, Daddy is tired this morning so we're going to go without him. He needs some extra sleep, don't you think?"

"No, I think he needs to go with us. He never does anything with us anymore. Doesn't he still love us?"

"Of course he loves you baby, more than anything in the world. Daddy has just been working a lot lately, but guess what?"

"What?"

"After church, we are going to Auntie Brook and Uncle Eric's house for a while so you can play with the kids, and then we are going to stop by and have dinner with Grandma and Granddaddy."

"Okay Mommy, let's hurry up and go." Kaylie sang as she pushed her breakfast bowl away and jumped up from her chair.

Mia finished dressing Kaylie and then went to her room to put on her shoes and grab her purse.

"Where are you going?" David asked without bothering to open his eyes.

"Church."

"Why didn't you wake me up?"

"If I had, would you have gone?"

"Probably not, but it would have been nice to have been asked. Are ya'll coming straight home?"

"Nope, we're going to visit Brook for a bit and then having dinner with my parents."

"Well damn, what am I supposed to do all day and what the hell am I gonna eat."

"David, you're a grown man. You don't seem to have a problem figuring out what to do with your nights so I know you can find something to do today. Humph, you can take yourself out for dinner."

"Whatever. Tell my baby I love her."

"Why don't you drag yourself out of bed and tell her yourself. She's been asking why you don't spend time with us anymore and if you still love her. Don't you think you should go talk to her? Reassure her that you still love her?"

Without another word, David got out of bed and went to talk with Kaylie. He approached her room and then stood in the doorway, watching his little girl play with her favorite doll.

"Good morning, princess."

"Daddy!" Kaylie squealed as she ran into her father's arms. "Daddy, are you coming with us? Please say yes, Daddy."

"Oh princess, I wish I could, but Daddy has some work that he has to finish. Plus I don't want to make you and Mommy late. You know how upset Mommy gets when she's late for church."

"Yeah, I know." Kaylie's expression had completely changed. She was now pouting and on the verge of tears.

"Princess, please don't cry. You know that daddy hates to see you cry."

"Then come with us."

"I can't, sweetie, but I tell you what, why don't I pick you up from school tomorrow and take you to the park and out to dinner? Just me and you and our favorite Mexican restaurant."

"Really Daddy?"

"Yes, princess, I promise. Okay?"

"Okay." Kaylie's joyful mood had returned. At her mother's request, she grabbed her Pretty Princess purse, kissed her dad goodbye, and left for church.

It had been a long and exhausting day. Church service, of course, was fabulously uplifting. It provided Mia with the strength she needed to make it through another week without pulling her hair out or killing her husband. Mia had been praying day in and day out for God to fix her situation, but today, she changed her prayer. Today, Mia began to ask God to reveal His will for her life. She asked Him to make it painfully obvious to her what she should do about her marriage. At this point, Mia didn't care about how much she might be hurt by David's actions; she just needed to know what was going on in his life.

At dinner, Mia's mom had advised her not to go looking for anything or trying to dig up dirt on David. In her words, "When you looking for stuff, you usually find more than you bargained for." While Mia respected her mom's advise, there was no way she was going to follow it. There was no way Mia was going to allow herself to be blindsided by whatever David was doing. She didn't like being the fool and wasn't about to be a fool for her husband.

Naturally David was gone when Mia and Kaylie finally

returned home. Mia was actually glad for his absence this time. She'd been able to get Kaylie settled into bed, take a shower, and get in bed herself. Mia was all ready to settle in with a good book when the phone rang.

"Hello."

"Is this the Purcell residence?"

"Yes it is, how may I help you?"

"My name is Zoe and I thought it only fair that I inform you that your husband is cheating on *us*."

"Excuse me! What do you mean cheating on us?"

"Well, Mia, David and I started seeing one another shortly after the death of your baby. I've always encouraged him to stay with you. I was cool when it was just the two of us, but I be damned if I sit back and pretend that it's okay for him to see someone else."

Mia sat straight up in the bed unable to believe what she was hearing. And this woman had the nerve to address her by name as if they were old friends.

"Mia, are you there?"

"Yes, I'm here. What did you say your name was again?"

"Zoe. Zoe Miller."

"Well, Zoe, I can't believe you found the audacity to call my house and tell me that you've been screwing my husband for years. And you're now upset because he's cheating with yet another person. What do you want from me, sympathy? Do you want me to team up with you and confront David or something? Please let me know what you had in mind when you picked up the phone to call me because I'm really struggling to understand what you expect from me."

"I expected you would be grateful."

"Grateful for what?"

"For me exposing your husband for the dog he is. Grateful to know what he's been doing behind your back and honestly, our confronting him wouldn't be such a bad idea."

Mia listened to everything this crazy woman had to say and realized that her prayer had just been answered.

"You know Zoe, I am grateful. Well maybe I should say appreciative. I appreciate your letting me know the truth about my husband. Your reasons for doing so were completely wrong but, I appreciate the information none-the-less. Now, I'm going back to bed. Goodnight."

"Wait, don't hang up. What are we going to do about David?"

"I don't give a damn what you do about David. What happens with you two is none of my concern. Don't ever pick up the phone to call me again. Goodnight."

Mia hung up the phone and contemplated her next move. She leaned back on her pillows for a second and then reached for her purse and pulled out a business card. Adam Burch, Private Investigator was the name printed on the card. Mia grabbed the phone and dialed the number printed underneath the name.

"This is Adam."

"Hello Mr. Burch. My name is Mia Purcell. We met about a week ago at an after work mixer in the lobby of the Bank of America building."

"Yes, Mia, I remember you. What can I do for you?"

"Well I know that you usually do work for corporations, but I was wondering if you ever take jobs for individuals?"

"Not usually, but I could make an exception for you. What are you trying to uncover?"

Mia hesitated as the reality of what she was about to do hit her like a ton of bricks. She couldn't believe that her marriage had come to this.

"I seem to be having some marital problems, Mr. Burch. One of my husband's mistresses just called to inform me that my he was cheating on *us*."

"You're kidding?"

"I wish I were. I would like to have him followed so that when we go to court, I'll be well prepared."

"I understand. I'll need to gather some information from you. Why don't I come downtown tomorrow around noon and we can discuss the details over lunch. Will that work for you?"

"Yes, Mr. Burch, that will be just fine and I appreciate you taking my case."

"No problem and please call me Adam. I'll see you tomorrow."

"Okay Adam. Goodnight."

Mia hung up the phone and got on her knees. She thanked God for His revelations and making it clear to her what steps she needed to take next. As she rose to her feet, Mia was overcome by a calm, peacefulness that only God could give her.

# CHAPTER SIXTEEN

Tameka woke up and rolled over to wrap her arms around Wayne but, to her surprise, he wasn't there. She'd fallen asleep late last night trying to stay up and wait for him to get in. Wayne had advised her that he'd be late. He and some guys from work were going to hang out and catch the game. Tameka wondered what the hell else he'd caught that had him out all damn night.

As Tameka got out of bed and began her morning routine, she heard the front door open and close. Her first instinct was to run up on Wayne and cuss his ass out and drill him about where he'd been. She instead decided to wait and see what kind of excuse he'd come to her with. As she patiently waited, Tameka went about the business of pulling out her clothes for work and starting the water for her shower.

"Good morning, babe, how are you?"

"I'm good," Tameka replied. "Just a little curious."

"Yeah, I figured you would be. I know I should've called, but I didn't want to wake you up."

"Okay, so where were you all night?"

"I ended up sleeping on Joe's couch. I couldn't get the car to start and no one had jumper cables. Joe lives right around the corner from where we were hanging out and offered me his sofa. Since I was a little tipsy, I took him up on his offer and waited until this morning to call AAA."

"I see."

"Baby, don't be upset."

Tameka opened the shower door, looked over her shoulder and with a smile she softly said, "I'm not upset sweetie." Then she stepped in the shower and watched Wayne as he turned and retreated into the bedroom. All Tameka could think was what a bullshit story he'd just tried to feed her. But it was cool because if it was the last thing she did, Tameka would find out where he really was and exactly what was going on with him.

Mia decided to go into the office a little late today. She felt the need to talk about her issues and had called Brook and asked her to meet for breakfast. Mia had dropped Kaylie off at school and was now sitting in a booth at the Flying Biscuit waiting for Brook to arrive. Just as she was losing herself in thought, Mia felt a tap on her shoulder.

"Good morning, sweetie." Brook leaned over and greeted her friend with a big hug.

"Good morning, Brook. Thanks so much for meeting me. I know you have a busy day ahead and have other things that you could be taking care of right now."

"Girl please, I'm never too busy for my sister. So what's up?"

Before Mia could begin to catch Brook up on everything, the waitress approached the table to take their orders. There was no need to even look over the menus. They both got their usual order of grits with chicken sausage and of course, biscuits.

While they waited for their food to arrive, Mia filled Brook in on the phone call she'd received the night before. She didn't leave out a thing and could tell by the expression on Brooks face that she was dumbfounded by the news.

"Oh my goodness, Mia. You have got to be kidding me. Please tell me you're joking."

"Child please, do I look like I'm joking?"

"What did he say when you confronted him about all of this?"

"Brook, he still hadn't made it home when I left for work this morning. So even if I wanted to confront him this morning, it would have been impossible."

"Where is he?"

"Hell, I don't know. More importantly, I don't care."

"Well, Mia, I have to say that you seem awfully calm about the situation. What did you do, tear the house up in a rage last night or something? I know that I would be fit to be tied."

"No, girl, no rages for me. I had prayed for God to reveal to me what was going on with my husband, and He did. He answered my prayer, provided me with the means to take the next step to deal with all of this, and then Brook, my God gave me peace. I know that I'm going to be okay when this is all over."

"Wow. I…I don't even know what to say. I mean I'm glad that you're able to deal with this without freaking out, but what's next, Mia?"

Before Mia could respond, the waitress returned with their food, and Mia wasted no time digging in. Brook in her state of shock, played with her food more than she ate it. She was still trying to digest everything Mia had said.

"Brook, please eat your food. I promise I'm going to be okay. I just needed to say all of this out loud. I needed you to know what's going on. And to answer your question, my next step is to have David followed. I'm meeting with a private investigator today. I need to be fully prepared when we go to court."

"So we're definitely talking divorce?"

"Absolutely."

# CHAPTER SEVENTEEN

The past week had been a busy and lonely one for Brook. Eric had been out of town all week on business, so she had the kids and the company to handle alone. Of course they had a small office staff, but she was the decision maker, the head honcho. It was times like these that made her appreciate her husband more than usual.

Thank goodness, it was Friday and Brook's man was on his way home. She had gotten the kids fed, bathed, and in bed for the night. They were sleeping like little angels, a sharp contrast to earlier when they were behaving like Satan's spawn. Brook had helped the housekeeper with the cleaning in an effort to get her out of the house as soon as possible. Now, there were candles, fresh fruit, and Champaign in their bedroom. The only thing left to do was for Brook to decide what to wear.

As the garage door went up, Brook descended the stairs to greet her man. Eric walked through the door and saw his wife waiting for him with open arms. But in that ultra short, black, lace chemise she was wearing, her arms were the last parts of her body that he was thinking about. Without saying a word, Eric dropped his bags, grabbed his wife, and lifted her to his waist. She wrapped her legs around him and kissed him deeply. With her ass in his hands, he carried her up to their room.

The music played softly and the candles flickered as Eric laid Brook on the bed and slowly took off his clothes. She loved nothing more than to watch this fine ass man strip naked. He slowly moved his hands up her thighs and under her gown and lifted it over her head. Eric took his time looking at every inch of his wife. He leaned over her and began kissing her neck. He caressed her body as his mouth found its way to her mountain peaks. Her hardened nipples turned him on and brought her great pleasure as well. It wasn't long before his face was buried between her legs. She became wetter and moaned more seductively with every lick of his tongue. And the suction she felt drove her insane. When she thought she could take no more, Eric lifted her legs to his shoulders and slid his strong manhood inside of her. The intensity of their love making was unbelievable. Twenty minutes later, they collapsed into an exhausted heap.

After cuddling and whispering sweet nothings for a while, Eric decided that he was hungry. The two got up, wrapped themselves in bathrobes and headed downstairs. Brook pulled out some leftover pasta salad and barbeque chicken. She fixed up a nice plate for Eric and retrieved him a beer from the refrigerator.

"How did you know I wanted a beer?"

"Because I know my man. Besides, you always like a cold beer with barbeque. So did you get everything taken care of with that deal, or will you have to leave me again to tie it all up?"

"Nope, I got the deal sealed up like a drum and managed to get us an even bigger financial cut than we originally thought."

"Oh baby, you're the man."

"And you know it. So did I miss anything while I was gone making that money?"

"Did you ever! Did you know that your friend, David, has been having an affair?"

"Honestly, Brook, I don't have a clue as to what has been going on with David. I haven't really been talking with him much. When I have called, he's rushed me off the phone with promises of calling me back, but of course, he never does. How do you know he's having an affair?"

"Mia told me. She received a phone call from some chick named Zoe. Apparently, David has been seeing Zoe for years, and now she's upset that he's also seeing someone else. She actually had the nerve to tell Mia that David was cheating on them. Can you believe that? What kind of mess is that?"

"Oh damn, that's messed up. How is Mia holding up?"

"She seems to be okay with everything. She has decided to go ahead and file for divorce. I know that she's hurt. She wouldn't be human if she wasn't. I just hope that she continues to be strong and stay focused on her and Kaylie's well being."

"Well, I know that you let Mia know that we are here for her. I hate that she has to deal with this bullcrap, but I'm really not surprised. David has always had a wondering eye. I hate that I'm the one that brought him to Christmas dinner to meet her. She wouldn't be hurting now if I hadn't made that introduction."

"Baby, that was so long ago. They had some good years together. But, Mia deserves so much more than this."

"Yes, she does, and she will eventually find someone worthy of her love and affection. But right now, I want to give you the love that you deserve." Eric moved around to the side of the kitchen island that Brook was leaning on and pressed his body against hers. He kissed his wife and then turned her around so that her back was to him. He kissed her neck as he opened her robe and let it drop to the floor. Eric moved his hand to Brook's crotch and began to fondle her. She moaned with delight. The next thing she knew, she was being bent over the counter and Eric was entering her from behind. His forcefulness excited her to no end. Brook gripped the large slab of granite and threw those pelvic thrusts right back to him. The intensity was insane. Brook was elated to have her husband back home.

# CHAPTER EIGHTEEN

Tameka had enjoyed another week of working at the station. It felt so good to be contributing to something meaningful again. Her supervisor seemed to be really pleased with her work and was giving her more responsibility as the weeks rolled on. And this time around, Tameka had decided to take what the station offered her instead of trying to steal the positions she felt she deserved. It was a new day and she was going to follow the rules, at least where work was concerned.

Now, the work day had ended and Tameka had personal business to attend to. Wayne was about to leave his office for an evening meeting, and she wanted to know who this meeting was with. Tameka patiently waited outside of Wayne's office in her rental car. After about twenty minutes, the front door swung open and out walked Wayne. He was obviously in a hurry, he practically ran to his car. Tameka let him get about a car length away and pulled out behind him. She couldn't wait to see what their final destination would be.

Tameka maneuvered through traffic, careful not to tip Wayne off that she was hot on his trail. Her curiosity grew stronger once she followed him into a condominium complex. They were nice homes but not too upscale or over the top.

Wayne parked his car in front of a bank of condos located in the rear of the complex. Tameka observed him as he ascended the stairs and used a key to gain entrance into the door to the right. She had no idea how long he would be, so she backed the car into a space across from the building, kicked off her shoes, and settled in to wait.

Two hours later, the door to the residence opened and out walked Wayne. This time, he was moving at a much more casual pace. There seemed to be a spring in his step. He was clearly happy. Tameka put her shoes on, preparing to follow him but, something told her to wait. So as Wayne pulled away, Tameka patiently waited to see who else might emerge from the condo. Her wait was not in vain. Twenty minutes later, David appeared. He was accompanied by a short, thin female with a faded hair cut and the swagger of a dude. Tameka immediately jumped to the conclusion that this was David's mistress. She couldn't believe that this was the type of woman that David would choose to cheat with. The woman before her couldn't touch Mia's beauty or sophistication. Tameka raised her camera and snapped a picture. Today's investigation didn't yield the answers she was looking for but instead, raised more questions.

Mia was waiting patiently for Adam to join her for dinner at Houston's. She'd allowed him to convince her that this was just a business dinner, and there was no reason for her to be concerned about what others might think. She had to admit that he had a good point. Besides, David didn't give a crap about what his own wife thought about his behavior, let alone other folks. And if this was the fastest way for Mia to find out what David was up to, then so be it.

"Hello there," Adam spoke as he gently placed his hand on Mia's shoulder. "I hope you haven't been waiting long?"

"Not at all. Please, have a seat." Mia directed by pointing

towards the chair across from her. Do you have any information for me?"

"Yes, I do, but can I order a drink first? I know you're anxious, but dang woman, slow your roll." Adam chuckled in a deep, sexy voice.

The waiter approached their table and asked to take their order. Adam decided to take charge and order for the both of them. How he knew exactly what Mia wanted was beyond her, but he got her desired entrée exactly right. Even down to the salad dressing on the side. Mia was impressed but not moved.

"Okay Adam, now that you've ordered how about telling me what you've discovered as far as David is concerned?"

"Of course." Adam reached into his briefcase and pulled out a large envelope. "These were taken a couple of days ago." Adam pulled some pictures from the envelope and laid them on the table before Mia.

Mia hesitantly picked up the pictures and began to thumb through them. She saw her husband entering a condo with a short, thin woman. They seemed to know each other well. There were other pictures of the two of them in the mall, the park, and standing outside of David's car. The woman didn't look at all to be his type. She looked too tom-boyish for David's liking. But at this point, nothing would surprise Mia. She obviously didn't know his type anymore.

"Well Adam, while these photos are interesting, they don't really prove anything. There isn't one intimate shot of them. I need something that I can really use in court."

"Yes, I know. I'm working on it. Either they are really good friends, or they are being very careful. Either way, I promise, I'll get you what you need."

"Don't make promises you can't keep, Adam."

"I never do, Mia. Now, how about we enjoy dinner?" Adam quizzed as the waiter placed their order on the table.

"Well, let's dig in. After all, everything looks so good."

"You got that right." Adam shot back with a sly grin.

It had been a couple of days since Mia's meeting with Adam. She was very curious as to whether he'd discovered anything new about her husband. David was still coming and going from their home as if he lived alone. His only genuine interaction was with their daughter. Beyond that, he had nothing to say or anything to do with Mia. It was obvious to Kaylie that something was wrong between her parents, but since no one offered an explanation, she decided to pretend like all was okay with the world.

"Mommy, where are we going again? Over to Auntie Brook's house? When can we leave?"

"Yes, Kaylie, we're going to Auntie Brook's house, and we'll be leaving in just a minute. You must really be excited about your visit?"

"I am, Mommy. I always have fun over there. I hope the babysitter is there today. She is lots of fun."

"Well, it's your lucky day because she is there. And Kaylie, I want you to have fun but mostly, I want you to behave. Do you understand me?"

"Yes ma'am."

"Good, that's my big girl. Now grab your sweater and let's go."

It wasn't long before Mia and Kaylie were ringing the doorbell at Brook's house. As soon as the door opened, Kaylie jumped into Eric's arms.

"Hello, precious, how are you?" Eric asked in a very animated voice.

"I'm doing good Uncle Eric. I didn't know you were going to be here."

"I waited around just to say hello to you. Oh, and your mommy."

"Gee, thanks," Mia giggled.

"Come on in Mia." Eric greeted her with a hug. "Brook will

be down in a second and now that I have said hello, I'm off to play golf. Y'all have fun today."

Brook made her way down stairs just as Eric was turning to leave. He stopped long enough to hug and kiss his wife goodbye, and then he was gone. Brook turned and greeted Kaylie and Mia, then it was Kaylie's turn to rush out and join the other children in the play room. Brook and Mia gave final instructions to the babysitter and left for a day of female bonding.

The ladies headed to Buckhead in Brook's Range Rover. As they maneuvered through the city streets, the conversation flowed.

"Did I tell you that I met with Adam the other day?"

"Mia, who in the world is Adam?"

"Come on now, Brook. I told you that I hired a private investigator to get the goods on David. Don't you remember?"

"No, you told me that you were going to hire someone, but I didn't know that you had actually done it. Did he come highly recommended?"

"Yes, he did, and he's a really kind man."

"Well, what does he look like?"

"Girl, no one is trying to look at that man, at any man. I'm not paying attention to his appearance. All of my concentration is on taking care of my child and making sure that she and I are happy and secure."

"You like him," Brook snickered.

"Get a grip, I don't like him. I don't even like men in general right now. Besides, that's not where my head is. My mind is on getting the goods on David."

"Mia, I understand all that. But please just try and give me a general description of the man?"

"Umm, he's about six feet, two inches tall. He has the most beautiful, smooth, chocolaty complexion and he is very cut. Not bulky, but fit, fine, cut, nice."

"Well damn, that was very descriptive for someone not paying attention to his appearance."

"Whatever, Brook."

"Has he discovered anything new about David?"

"Girl, he came to our first meeting equipped with photos. They were shots of David with another woman. But, she didn't look at all like his type, Brook. To be perfectly honest, she looked a lot like a lesbian."

"Well, what were they doing, Mia?"

"Nothing really. They were hanging out at some sports bar. They weren't holding hands or kissing or anything. They looked like a couple of buddies hanging out after work."

"Maybe that is all there was to it. They are probably no more than friends."

"That's pretty much what I told Adam. Then I advised him that he had to do better than that and get me some information that I can use in court. I'm hoping to hear back from him soon. I am so ready to put this chapter of my life behind me. I'm eager to be done with David and all of his drama."

Brook whipped the car into a parking space right in front of Phipps Plaza. The ladies exited the vehicle and made their way through the parking lot. They were almost to the front doors when Mia heard someone call her name. She and Brook stopped in their tracks and turned around. To their surprise and disappointment, it was Tameka yelling for Mia. Brook and Mia looked at one another as if to ask "What the hell does she want?"

"Mia, I'm glad I saw you. I think I may have some information that may be of importance to you."

"Tameka, I can't imagine that anything you say would be of interest or importance to me. So why don't you keep your little information and leave us alone."

"Fine, Mia, I was just trying to be helpful. From now on, I'll ignore whatever I discover about your husband. Goodbye." Tameka turned and started to walk away.

"I can't believe I'm doing this," Mia mumbled. "Tameka, wait. Please tell me what information you have."

Tameka turned around and re-approached her old associates.

"I was actually checking on Wayne. I don't know what's up with him lately but anyway, I followed him to this condo," Tameka babbled as she pulled out pictures of the property. "I saw Wayne run in, and a couple hours later, he comes out looking as happy as a lark. I started to leave behind him but decided to wait a few more minutes. It wasn't long before I saw David emerge with this kind of hard looking woman." Tameka fumbled for a second and then pulled out more pictures. "You can have these if you like."

"Why are you giving me these, Tameka? Why are you involving yourself in my life?"

"Look, I'm not trying to get all up in your business or be a part of anyone's life. I have my own life, a new life, thank you. But when I saw this, I thought you'd want to know. I have questions about David and Wayne's new found friendship and what their business with one another is. I don't know how this chick fits into any of it. I simply thought that you'd have some of the same questions. So you can have those pictures. Goodbye."

Tameka turned on her heels and marched off. To Mia's surprise, she found herself running after Tameka. "Hey, wait a second, Tameka. Did you see any kind of intimacy between David and this girl?"

"No, just a lot of laughter and a hug. Bye." Tameka got in her car and was gone.

Mia slowly walked back over to Brook with pictures in hand. Again, the photos didn't reveal anything incriminating, but David seemed to enjoy himself while in this woman's company. Was he in love with her?

"Are you okay, Mia?

"Yeah, I'm fine. Can we walk back to the car for a minute so I can put this crap in there?"

"Absolutely, let's go."

The two returned to the car in silence. Mia opened her door and laid the pictures down. She took one last glance at them and began to cry. Brook went to comfort her friend.

"Come on, Mia, let's go eat first. We'll come back here later." Brook closed the door once Mia was situate inside and then ran around to her side of the car. By the time she started the car and pulled off, Mia's crying had transformed into heavy sobs. Brook pulled the vehicle around to a more secluded area of the parking lot. She jumped out and ran around to the passenger door. As soon as she got the door open, Mia fell into her arms, weeping.

"Oh my God, Brook. I can't believe any of this. This was never supposed to be my life. It was never supposed to be like this." Mia forced the words out in between sobs. "What the hell is wrong with me? Why am I not enough for David? What happened? What did I do to make him stop loving me?"

"Mia, none of this is your fault. You have been a wonderful wife to that man. What he is doing is a reflection of his poor character and has nothing to do with the type of woman or wife you have been. I don't ever want to hear you blaming yourself."

"Brook, I had to do something to push him away. I just think that I could deal with all of this better if I knew what I did."

"Sweetheart, I promise you, you did nothing. David obviously has issues that are so far beyond anything that we could comprehend. He's the one that did this; he's the responsible party, not you."

Brook held her friend for a few moments longer and then reached into the glove box for tissues. She tried to help Mia wipe away the smeared mascara that streaked down her face. Mia's make-up officially looked a hot mess.

# CHAPTER NINETEEN

Two days later, Tameka found herself still annoyed with Mia. Hell, Tameka was trying to be helpful, despite their past and utter dislike for one another. And she didn't even want to think about Brook. That bitch still had her little holier than thou attitude. There was no way that Tameka would demean herself by attempting to speak to Brook again. Her position now was, screw Brook and the horse she rode in on.

Traffic was pretty heavy for it to be so early in the afternoon. But Tameka endured as she made her way through town to Connie's office. She of course had to keep all of her scheduled appointments but was torn as to whether she would share with Connie everything that had been going on. Connie had been a great listener and provided excellent feedback and advice so far, but how would she receive the things that Tameka had done lately? By the time Tameka reached the elevator in the office building, she'd decided to just let it all hang out. She hadn't broken any laws or hurt anyone, so the worst that Connie could do would be to shake a finger at her and scream "stop".

"Come on in, Tameka. I'm so sorry I had to reschedule our meeting last week. It really couldn't be helped."

"It's okay. It worked out well for me, gave me a chance to

take care of some things." Tameka replied as she took a seat in the over-sized chair across from Connie.

"So, how have the last week and a half been for you? Is work still going well?"

"Oh yes, I absolutely love my job, Connie. They are giving me more and more responsibility and are even letting me do a little production work."

"That is fabulous. Are they letting you produce a particular spot? I need to know what to look for."

"Let's not get crazy. I'm co-producing a small spot on the state's lake levels as it pertains to last year's drought."

"That's really great, Tameka. Today co-producer, tomorrow producer. But, you're going to let them bestow that honor on you. You're not going to try and force it by destroying the one that holds the job now, right?"

"No, I'm so far beyond that it's not even funny. Those days are behind me. I will not be repeating those mistakes again."

"Well, I'm glad to hear that. Now tell me, what else has been going on? How are things with you and Wayne?"

"Things for me are confused."

"What do you mean?"

Tameka got up and walked over to the window. She looked out over the city and watched the cars fly up and down the interstate as she contemplated how much she would tell Connie. Then she thought, screw it. May as well tell it all. "I found myself following Wayne the other day."

"I'm listening."

"He has been acting so strange lately. He's still loving and attentive when he's home. The problem is that he is never home for long. There is always a meeting, a new client, beers after work, something, anything, everything to pull him away from me. He now keeps extra clothes in his car at all times. That kind of stuff will worry you to death. So I decided to follow him."

"Tameka, that could be so dangerous. Are you sure you want to be playing detective?"

"I can't afford a real one, so yes; I have to do it myself. I don't want to hurt anyone or cause any problems, but if there is another woman, I need to know. Wayne has been so good to me. He stuck with me through so much, and I will be there for him. If he's going through something, having difficulties, I'm there for him. But I will not share him with another woman. If I'm no longer what he wants, if he is happy with someone else, I will let him go. I love him enough to do that, but I won't be made a fool of."

"So did you uncover his deep, dark secret?"

"No, but I did discover that whatever he is doing, David Purcell is either part of it or aware of it."

"Purcell…any relation to Mia?

"Yes. It's her husband."

"Oh, I see. And why do you say that he's aware of what's going on?"

Tameka proceeded to share with Connie what she saw. She even went on to tell her about the encounter with Mia and how she felt about it after the fact.

"And how did you feel about Brook and the fact that you all didn't speak?"

"That heffa isn't even on my radar anymore. To hell with her. I've paid my debt, and if that's not enough for her, then that's her damn problem." Tameka snapped as she made her way back to her seat.

"Tameka, I want you to be careful. Not only with your detective work but with what you choose to share with Mia. I'm sure she knows that there may be something off with her marriage, but she doesn't need you stirring the pot. This is a situation that could potentially blow up in your face. You don't want to be responsible for the break-up of someone else's relationship, and you don't want Wayne catching you playing detective. Heed my warning. You may think you can handle whatever you manage to unearth but, you don't know what you're dealing with or how you'll react when it all comes to a head. Be careful. Please re-consider what you are doing."

"I hear you. I will take your advice to heart. Now, if I'm not mistaken, that's my time. So, smooches and I'll see you next week."

# CHAPTER TWENTY

Several days had passed since Mia and Brook had their little parking lot meeting with Tameka. Brook hadn't been able to decide if Tameka was really just passing on information or if she was up to something dirty. She was pleased that Tameka hadn't uttered a word to her. Brook wanted no type of exchange with the woman; however, she didn't want Mia getting tangled up with her either. Brook didn't care how much time Tameka had spent in prison or how much therapy she had received. In Brook's eyes, Tameka was still and always would be a crazy ass psycho. She'd have to do what she could to protect Mia from the dangers that came with dealing with Tameka. But protecting Mia could mean inviting Tameka back into her life.

"Babe, what's got you in such a daze? You're sitting there staring off into space," Eric quizzed.

"I don't know, Eric. I'm concerned about Mia, and I'm really worried about Tameka's need to share information with Mia about what's going on with David. I don't get why she felt the need to give Mia the pictures or share what she saw. There has to be some ulterior motive, but, what is it?"

"Brook, you can stop this bull right now. I will not have you being involved with that bitch again. I don't want her talking to you, bumping into you, nothing. If Mia chooses to deal with her, then that's on Mia, but you are to have no involvement. Do you hear me?"

"Well who the hell are you now, James Evans? Next you're gonna tell me that my place is in the bedroom and the kitchen. You don't have to speak to me in that manner, and you know I don't react well to orders."

"You know what? You can try to change this crap up all you want but, the fact of the matter is Tameka is a crazy bitch. She's killed our child, killed an innocent man, and ruined the lives of others just for fun. So I would think that common sense would tell you to stay the hell away from her."

"I know I need to stay away from her, and I've made that clear to Tameka. I told her in no uncertain terms to stay the hell away. But am I supposed to just let Mia get caught up with her? Mia is in a very fragile state right now and obviously needs me to help direct her away from those that don't have her best interest at heart."

"I realize that Mia is your girl and that you want to protect her, but do you realize that you weren't able to protect yourself from Tameka?"

"Yes, I realize that, and I really don't have any plans to get tangled up with Tameka again. I will be observing from a distance, just watching Mia's back."

"Fine, Brook. But don't say I didn't warn you, and don't put me in a position of having to kill that heffa as a means of protecting you."

"There will be no need for you to commit murder, Eric. Trust me, I'm dealing with the situation from a distance. It will be fine."

Both Eric and Brook grabbed their things and headed out for the day. Brook had errands to run and items to pick up for the kids. But first, she had to head across town for a business meeting. It was mid-morning so traffic wasn't too bad. It was a gorgeous day but, the thought of having to sit through another sponsorship presentation didn't excite Brook at all. With the economy spiraling down, she and Eric's firm was actually trying to pull back on sponsorship dollars, but non-profits and other organizations kept asking anyway.

Brook turned into the parking lot, surveyed the small building, and parked. She grabbed her briefcase and headed for the door. As she approached the front desk, she began to feel uneasy, weird. She couldn't put her finger on it; it was like she was expecting something un-pleasant to happen.

"Hello, I have a meeting with…" Before she could finish her statement, Patricia stepped around the corner and cheerfully greeted Brook.

"Good morning, Mrs. Mansfield-Banks. So nice to see you again."

"Thank you, Mrs. Gillman. Good to see you as well. And please call me Brook."

"Only if you'll call me Patricia."

"It's a deal."

"Well Brook, if you'll follow me, we will get this meeting underway. My staff is very excited about seeing you. I have a couple of new employees that I'd like for you to meet as well."

"Wonderful. Lead the way."

The ladies made their way to the conference room where the small staff was gathered. Everyone was very warm and welcoming, and Brook smiled broadly as she shook each person's hand. But when she looked up into the face of the next employee, she was shocked. It was Tameka. Patricia stepped forward to make the formal introduction.

"Brook, I would like for you to meet the newest addition to our staff, Tameka Williams. She comes to us with a lot of television experience and is proving to be quite valuable to this organization."

Tameka extended her hand. "So nice to meet you, Mrs. Mansfield-Banks."

Stunned, Brook accepted Tameka's hand and babbled, "Nice to meet you, Ms. Williams."

"If you all would excuse us, Mrs. Mansfield-Banks and I need to get to business. Holly, please prepare Mrs. Mansfield-Banks' coffee to her liking and grab us some water as well. Thank you."

Brook's eyes stayed on Tameka as she and the rest of the staff made their exit. Now Brook knew what that uneasy feeling was all about.

Patricia went on with her presentation, effectively speaking about how Brook's sponsorship would help keep quality programming on public television. Patricia made valid points, but Brook barely heard them. Her mind was on Tameka. She couldn't figure out for the life of her why someone as smart and savvy as Patricia would allow herself to be fooled by the likes of Tameka. How had Tameka convinced Patricia to hire her?

The presentation had ended and a portfolio of information had been given to Brook to reference while she and Eric debated the possible release of funds to the station. As Brook headed toward the front of the building, she spotted Tameka in her cubicle and decided to go and have a word with her.

Patricia, would you mind if I speak to your new employee for a second?"

"Not at all, I'll wait here for you and then see you to the door."

"Thank you." Brook replied. Then she walked back to Tameka. "How did you manage to snag this position?"

"Does it really matter, Brook?"

"You're right, I don't care about that. But I do care about your interaction with Mia. She has her hands full right now and does not need any foolishness from you. So stay away from Mia. She doesn't need your counsel when it comes to her marriage and she does not need your pictures. She can handle things without input from the peanut gallery."

"Brook, I'm going to say this as nicely as I can. Back up off me; stay out of my face and my business. What I do and say and to whom I do and say it is none of your concern. You wanted me to leave you alone, and I will. Now, you need to leave me alone. Goodbye."

"I'm warning you Tameka, stay out of Mia's business." Brook turned and walked away.

"I didn't realize that you already knew Tameka?" Patricia inquired.

"Oh no, I just had a question. Well, thank you Patricia, you've given me a lot to think about. I'll be in touch soon with our decision."

"Thank you, Brook. I look forward to hearing from you."

After Brook had left the building, Patricia made her way to Tameka's desk. "Tameka, what did Brook want to ask you?"

"Humph, she thought she knew me from somewhere. But she was confused, she doesn't know me at all," Tameka retorted.

## CHAPTER TWENTY-ONE

Tameka left work and headed home. It had been a long day, a disturbing day. She was still trying to figure out when Brook had grown a set of balls. She was usually so meek and non-threatening, but today she decided to warn Tameka. Tameka couldn't help but laugh a little because she knew that she would mop the damn floor with Brook. But when the brief moment of laughter ended, Tameka's mind drifted to what devious things she could do to show Brook who was really the bad ass.

Tameka was surprised to see Wayne's car in the driveway. She assumed he would be out for the evening. She took a deep, cleansing breath and made her way in the house. As she closed the door behind her, she was shocked at what awaited her inside. There were candles everywhere. Soft music played in the background, and Wayne was busy in the kitchen preparing dinner. Tameka dropped her tote bag and stood with her mouth gaped open.

"Hey Babe, I didn't hear you come in. How was your day?" Wayne asked as he wrapped Tameka up in his arms.

"Um, hey. What's going on here? I figured you'd be out for the night."

"Well, I haven't been around as much as I should lately, so I decided to do something nice while begging your forgiveness."

"Interesting. What's for dinner?"

"To be honest, I cheated. I only made the salad. The rest came from Maggiano's."

"Nice."

"Everything is ready. Why don't you come on and have a seat? I'll pour you a glass of wine and then fix your plate. You are hungry, right?"

"Yes, it's been a long day, and I skipped lunch. I'm sure I'll enjoy this. What did you get?"

"Your favorite, lasagna."

"Great. Let me go to the bathroom and wash up. I'll be right back."

Tameka returned and took a seat at the table. Wayne served her as if it was what he did daily to earn a living. Tameka was further surprised by Wayne's constant conversation. She couldn't remember the last time he was this talkative. She also found it interesting that all they discussed were shallow topics, nothing of any substance. When she tried to delve into deeper conversation, like what he'd been doing with his evenings, he would instantly change the subject.

The food was delicious and Tameka loved that she wasn't the one cleaning up after the meal. She just sat and watched as Wayne went about the business of cleaning up the dishes and putting away the left-over food. She couldn't help but wonder why Wayne was so evasive when she asked the simplest questions. He absolutely didn't want to talk about himself. Tameka wondered if his lack of conversation was his way of not letting some deep, dark secret slip out by mistake. She still hadn't figured out this new found friendship with David, and his behavior made her more curious than ever. Wayne was forcing her to keep her detective hat on. It was just a matter of time before she found out what was going on.

Tameka excused herself from the kitchen and made her way

to the bedroom. She disrobed, stepped into the bathroom, and ran a hot bubble bath. Once the tub was full and the jets were running, she slid into her perfect escape. Head resting on a bath pillow, body submerged in wet warmth, Tameka lay there wondering how she could possibly find out exactly what was up with her man. Hell, was he still her man? Did he plan a nice dinner in an effort to ease the guilt he was feeling for whatever it was he was doing? So many questions and not nearly enough answers. Wayne stepped to the side of the tub, startling her and snapping her out of constant state of wonder.

"Babe, want me to wash your back for you?" Wayne whispered softly.

"Yes, please. That would be nice."

Wayne lifted the bath cloth and covered it in body wash. He gently rubbed the towel over her back, top to bottom, side to side. Tameka seemed so relaxed that Wayne decided to continue. He washed every inch of her, slowly, gently, lovingly. He held her hands and helped her out of the tub, wrapped her in a towel and carried her to their bed. He gently laid her down, kissed her passionately, and loved her as if they would never get the chance again.

The next morning when Tameka awoke, she found herself alone. Wayne was nowhere to be found. He had obviously left before the crack of dawn. What in the world could possibly be going on? Tameka scratched her head, stretched her body, and got up to prepare for work. After work, she'd head to her therapy session and try to squeeze in a little detective work.

Having wrapped everything at work up a little early, Tameka headed for her weekly session. She wasn't feeling it today, didn't want to talk about nothing with nobody. But she appreciated her freedom too much now to start playing the no-show game. It didn't take long before she was face-to-face with her counselor.

"So, what's been going on, Tameka? How has this week been for you so far?"

"Stressful."

"Care to elaborate?"

"Not really."

"This is going to be a very long, drawn out session with this type of conversation."

"Look, Connie, I'm just not in the mood today. I'm tired, tired of thinking, wondering, contemplating. I'm just tired.'

"I can understand that, Tameka. But why don't you at least tell me what all the heavy thinking and contemplating is about?"

"What's it always about? Wayne. I swear he is driving me crazy. All the mystery surrounding him now. His disappearing acts and refusal to talk to me about what the hell is going on. And if all of that isn't enough, Brook had the nerve to try and confront me the other day. That bitch needs to step away before I decide to snap her head off."

"Please don't make threats? That kind of talk won't lead to anything good."

"Whatever."

"'So, what's up with Wayne?"

"That's what I'm trying to figure out. I've been doing a little detective work, but so far it's left me with more questions than answers."

"Tameka, I know I've said it before and now I'm going to say it again. I strongly suggest that you put the brakes on your little detective work. Nothing good will come of it."

"Answers, Connie, answers. That's what will come of it."

"And what if Wayne catches you spying on him or snooping through his things? Can't you see how that will only lead to more problems?"

"Maybe Connie, but things can't get much worse than they are now. I rarely see him. He's become best buds with this guy, David, and I see him creeping in and out of some woman's condo. Tell me, what else do you think I should be doing?"

"You should be communicating with him. I thought we discussed earlier how important it is to keep an open line of communication, no matter the type of relationship you're dealing with."

"Oh enough, Connie. Shut up with that communication bullshit! I can't get that man to speak about anything other than the weather. He won't even look me in the eye, let alone talk about what's happening in his life. He wants me to know nothing, understand nothing, about his dealings. And that is unacceptable!"

# CHAPTER TWENTY-TWO

It was late Friday afternoon and Mia was just not excited about the weekend. Her baby girl was spending the weekend with her parents, and she knew that her husband would not be around. It would be three nights full of loneliness. Mia gathered her things from her desk, grabbed her bag from her desk drawer, and headed out of the building. The only thing she really had to look forward to was her meeting with Adam tonight. They were scheduled to meet at 8:30 pm at Justin's for a little bite to eat and for Adam to share what he had learned about her husband.

As Mia rode down Ashford Dunwoody listening to the radio, she reached for her phone as it began to ring.

"Hello"

"Hi, Mia, this is Adam. How are you?"

"I'm fine. How are you, Adam?"

"I'm good. I do have a favor to ask you though. Would you mind if we reschedule for tomorrow evening? Something has come up that I really need to take care of."

"Oh, okay. We can certainly do this later; besides, I'm in no hurry for bad news."

"Are you sure tomorrow will work for you?"

"Yes, Adam, tomorrow will be fine. Just call me tomorrow

afternoon and give me specifics on where and when you want to meet."

"Will do. And Mia thanks for being so understanding."

"No problem. I'll talk with you later. Bye."

Mia hit the end button on her phone and her heart sank. As lame as it sounds, she was actually looking forward to dinner tonight. Not necessarily the news she would hear about David, but the idea of a good meal with a decent person in a nice atmosphere. Oh well, there's always tomorrow. As far as tonight was concerned, Mia decided on Chinese take-out and an On Demand viewing of *Seven Pounds*. By the time the food carton was empty and the movie was over, Mia was in tears. Why the hell couldn't she have chosen a comedy instead? Tomorrow couldn't come fast enough.

A positive attitude and busy day was what Mia woke up and decided to have. She would not allow herself to feel sorry for herself or cry about her situation. Mia decided to busy herself with housework in the morning and then an afternoon of shopping with Brook. Hopefully this trip to the mall would turn out better than the last. By 11:30 am, Mia's house was spotless and she was all dolled up and ready to go.

"Hey girl," Mia greeted Brook with a kiss on the cheek as Brook slid into the passenger seat.

"Hey yourself, how are you doing today?"

"I'm good, ready to get out here and partake in a little shopping therapy."

"I hear you, girl. Let's make it happen."

"So is Eric hanging out with the kids today?"

"He actually took them over to his parent's house. He and his father are going to go play a few holes of golf while his mom hangs out with the kids. She's been pestering us for more time with them, so today she gets her wish. I just hope that they don't drive Grandma insane."

"Now we both know that they won't. They are just happy to be there. Hell, I'd be happy to be there with the way that that woman cooks for them and lets them load up on sugar. I need a grandma to treat me like that."

"I told her if she gave them too much sugar, I was going to send her their dental bill. So hopefully she can show a little restraint today. So tell me, how was your dinner with Adam last night?"

"It was horrible because it got cancelled. So I ended up eating take out and watching *Seven Pounds*."

"That was the movie with Will Smith, right? How was it?" Brook inquired.

"Yes, it featured Will, and it was sad as hell. Everybody damn dying and here he is coughing up organs to try and save those he deemed as worthy. It was a good movie, but I was not in the right frame of mind to be watching anything like that last night."

"Mental note to self, don't watch that movie when I need cheering up." Brook chuckled. "So, Mia, have you and Adam rescheduled?"

"Yes, we're actually meeting tonight at Nan's. And while I'm not looking forward to what he has to say about my husband, I am looking forward to the meal. I've heard great things about that place."

"You'll have to let me know how it is; maybe Eric and I will go check it out if you say it's good. You know how picky you are, so if you enjoy it I'm sure we will."

Within three hours, the women had bought out Phipps Plaza, or at least tried to. They grabbed a quick bite to eat and then headed down the Georgia 400 toll road on their way to Perimeter Mall. It was, of course, the only mall in Atlanta with a MAC store. Mia was in desperate need of new eye shadows and a new tube of her favorite Viva Glam lip gloss. On their way to check out shoes in Nine West, Mia spotted Tameka waiting in line at the food court.

"Wait a minute, Brook. I see Tameka, and I need to ask her a quick question."

"Mia, you have a detective, you don't need that damn psycho."

"Brook, it's just a question. Don't worry, I remember well how pathological she is, and I won't get caught up with her. I promise it's only one question."

The women stepped to Tameka and if looks could kill, they both would have been dead on the spot. "What the hell do y'all want?"

"Hey, Tameka. I'm not here to bother you; I just have a quick question. Have you learned any more about this friendship between David and Wayne or observed any more suspicious behavior?"

"That's two questions and I suggest you get yourself a PI."

"I have one, but I'm asking you, Tameka. Really, it's a simple question."

"Look Mia, I'm going through the same mess you are with your man so I understand. I have seen him with the same woman but not in an intimate way. He and Wayne seem closer than ever, but I still haven't figured out what their connection is. That's all I know, and from now on, I think you need to rely on other sources for your information."

"I couldn't agree more," chimed Brook.

"Shut the hell up puppet master. No one is talking to your ass." Tameka retorted.

"Okay, stop it. Tameka, thank you for the information. I promise not to bother you anymore. Have a good day."

"Yeah, you too, Mia."

Brook and Mia walked away and picked up their route to the shoe store. They walked in silence for a couple of minutes as Mia played Tameka's words back in her head.

"Brook, hold up a minute. What did Tameka mean when she called you puppet master?"

Brook went on to tell Mia about her meeting at the television station and her subsequent warning to Tameka. And while Mia appreciated Brook's concern for her and her desire to protect her, she didn't want Brook shutting down any of her sources of information. Even if one those sources was the devil herself.

Within the hour, Mia had dropped Brook off at home and was headed home herself to prepare for her meeting tonight with Adam. She didn't really know why, but Mia found herself dawning a new pair of pants, new blouse that accentuated two of her best qualities, and strappy heels for her meeting. For some reason, she felt the need to look really nice tonight. Once she was dressed and make up had been applied, Mia double checked herself in the mirror and was pleased with the reflection. She turned and left for her evening out.

As she walked through the door of the restaurant, Mia spotted Adam seated at a table not too far from the front. She made her way to him and was pleased by the expression on his face when he stood to greet her.

"Well hello there. You look amazing tonight."

"Thank you, Adam. How are you tonight?"

"Just fine, thank you. Please have a seat." Adam pulled out a seat for Mia while he admired her view from behind. "I figured we could eat first and talk business after. Is that okay with you?"

Mia smiled warmly, "That will be just fine."

They dined on the delicious Thai cuisine and listened to the soft music that played in the background. They talked and laughed a little. Mia so enjoyed it that she now had no desire to discuss David at all. But, she knew it had to be done. With the table now cleared of food, the time was now upon them to get down to business.

"Well, Mia, are you ready to discuss what the investigation has revealed or would you rather have another cocktail with me and we save the business for tomorrow?"

"As tempting as that sounds, let's go ahead and discuss my husband and his affairs."

Adam reached for a business envelope that had been resting on the chair beside him. Without a word, he passed it to Mia.

She slowly opened the package and pulled out a few photos of David. In one he was greeting Wayne warmly at some bar. Another, he was with the young woman she'd previously found out about. They looked so close. The next one, he was standing with the woman and holding a little boy in his arms. The last photo, the little boy was affectionately kissing David. The boy could be her husband's twin.

"This is his son?" Mia asked as her voice cracked.

"Yes. He's twenty-one months old and lives with his mother in the condo where David spends so much time. I'm so sorry Mia."

"He went out and replaced our son." Tears were streaming down Mia's cheeks. "I have to go." Mia grabbed her purse and the pictures and ran for the door. Adam tried to stop her, but he was halted by the waiter waiving the check in his face.

Within minutes, Mia was flying down Interstate 20 crying like a baby. Her heart was broken, and the beating of it caused her physical pain. She tried wiping the tears away but they just kept flowing. In an effort to confirm that what she'd seen was true, she grabbed the picture of David and his son and looked at it once more. She didn't realize she was drifting into the other lane and the sound of a car horn startled her. She looked up, tried to correct the wheel but over compensated. The last thing she saw was the median wall coming towards her.

# CHAPTER TWENTY-THREE

The phone rang and Brook jumped at the sound. She sat up and glanced at the bedside clock. It read 2:45a.m., and her heart began to race. She hesitated only for a second and then grabbed the phone.

"Hello."

"I am so sorry for calling this late, but my name is Adam and I am an associate of Mia's. I found your number in her cell phone."

"What's wrong, Adam?"

"There's been an accident. Mia has been admitted to the hospital with some pretty serious injuries. I didn't know who else to call."

"Oh my goodness, I can't believe this. Okay, Adam, I'm on my way."

Brook jumped out of bed and began to get dressed as she filled Eric in on what had happened. She ran out of the house leaving Eric with the job of contacting David and advising him of the accident. As she drove the city streets at this ungodly hour, Brook contemplated if she should call Mia's parents or wait until she got to the hospital and uncovered more details. Brook's mind also drifted to the last time she rushed off when there was a car accident. Her parents both died, leaving her to pick up the pieces of her life. But Adam was clear when he said serious injuries. Her friend was not dead and for that, she was grateful. She decided to wait until she could find out Mia's condition before calling her parents.

Brook ran through the hospital doors and straight to the information desk. After receiving instructions on finding Mia's room, Brook took off in a hurry again. She found the room in no time at all, but paused for a moment before going in. She took several deep breaths in an effort to calm herself. She said a quick prayer and then entered her room. She eased up to Mia's bedside and caressed her friend's badly bruised face.

"Oh God, Mia, what happened, baby? How did this happen to you?" Brook whispered, knowing that her friend was in no condition to respond. Brook wasn't even sure if Mia had regained consciousness since being brought in. Just as Brook was turning to leave the room, the door opened slowly and a tall, ruggedly handsome man entered the room holding a cup of coffee.

"Hello, you must be Brook," the man said with an extended hand. "I'm Adam."

"Hi, Adam, it's nice to meet you. What can you tell me about the accident and Mia's condition now?"

"Unfortunately, I had some very disturbing news to share with Mia. She was so upset; she ran from the restaurant and sped off in her car. I took off behind her because I wanted to follow her home. You know, make sure she arrived safely, but she completely lost control of her car and hit the median wall on Interstate 20. I'm so sorry, I feel completely responsible."

"You shouldn't, Adam. You were only doing what Mia hired you to do and that was obtain information for her. Have you spoken with the doctors?"

Just as she asked the question, one of Mia's physicians entered the room. "Hello, I'm Dr. Burns. Are you her next of kin?"

Brook lied, "Yes, I'm her sister. How is she? What are her injuries?"

"Ma'am, your sister has suffered a pretty severe concussion. She also has a couple of cracked ribs as well as a broken leg. Now the break was a clean break and should heal with no problem, we've bandaged her ribs tightly and they should heal without a problem as well. Our greatest concern is the concussion. Head injuries are always of great concern for us. We will monitor her closely, and it is our hope that she regains consciousness soon. Once she does, we'll have a better opportunity to assess her mental state. Of course, the sooner she wakes, the less chance there will be for any permanent damage. Are there any other questions I can answer for you?"

"Yes, is there anything that I can do that might help her come around?"

"You can talk to her. Talk to your sister and let her know that you're here with her. Make sure she knows that she is not alone. You would be surprised how much of what you say is actually heard by the patient."

"Okay, Dr. Burns. Thank you so much."

"You're quite welcome, and I'll be back to check on her soon."

As the doctor turned to leave the room, Brook returned to Mia's bedside. She gently lifted Mia's hand to her lips and kissed it. "I'm here, girl. I'm here and I love you." Brook then turned her attention to Adam "I need to call her parents. Can you stay with her for just a few minutes more while I make a couple of calls?"

"Brook, I'm not going anywhere. Take your time. She won't be alone."

Brook stepped out of the room and called Mia's parents. She tried explaining what had happened in between the screams of panic coming from Mia's mom. She assured them that Mia wasn't alone and that the doctor felt certain that Mia would make a full recovery. Mia's parents didn't want Kaylie to see her mom like that and decided that they would take turns coming to the hospital. Mia's mom would be the first to arrive. The next call was to Eric, Brook was curious as to whether he'd been able to reach David or not. Eric advised her that he'd called several times and left messages for David, but he had yet to receive a response. Why was Brook not surprised?

When Brook reentered the hospital room, she was surprised to see Adam sitting at Mia's side, holding her hand. She stood back and quietly observed for a minute. "I'm so sorry, Mia" she heard him say. "If I could do it all over, I don't know that I would've shared those photos with you. You are too good to be treated the way you have been. I'm so sorry." He kissed her hand and laid it back on the bed. He was so gentle and showed so much concern for Mia. It made Brook wonder if he wanted to be more to Mia than just her hired help.

"Adam, you must be tired. Mia's mom is on her way, and I'm not going to leave any time soon. You can take off if you want to."

"Maybe a little later. Were you able to reach her husband?"

"My husband Eric has called him and left several messages, but no response yet."

"That son-of-a-bitch."

"Adam, what information did you share with Mia that got her so upset?"

"I wish I could tell you Brook, I really do. But I have to honor client confidentiality no matter what."

"I understand."

It wasn't long before Mia's mother arrived. She and Brook held vigil at Mia's bedside. They took turns holding her hand and talking to her about everything under the sun. Adam had left and gone home for a little rest. He returned to the hospital around 7:00p.m. to relieve Brook and Mia's mom. He assured them that he would not leave Mia's side. It was his intension to spend the night holding her hand.

Midnight was when Adam was awakened by the feel of

something stroking his face. It was Mia's hand. Adam lifted his head and smiled as if he'd just won the lottery. "You're awake. Thank God, you're awake. Let me get the doctor, I'll be right back." Adam jumped and ran to the nurse's desk. He immediately returned to the room and took his place at Mia's side. It wasn't long before the on-call physician entered the room and did a brief evaluation. With a smile on his face, he advised that everything looked good. They would send Mia for a CAT scan to be sure but expected for it to come back normal. Adam could not have been happier.

# CHAPTER TWENTY-FOUR

It had been three days since the accident, and Mia was still in the hospital. She was so thankful to be alive. She was very sore but the doctors and nurses were insistent on her getting up and moving around. They wanted to see her up and down the hall on those crutches. She was grateful for her parents and Brook; they had been there for her in a really big way. She hadn't been left alone for more than a minute or two since being admitted. Surprisingly, Adam had been there for her as well. He was the friend that took the night shift. He was with her each night, all night. There was only one person missing, her husband. David had not even bothered to return any of Eric or her parents' phone calls. He had not called one time to check on his injured wife. If Mia had any doubts before about David's lack of love for her, she didn't anymore. She knew beyond any shadow of a doubt that his love for her was dead and gone.

Brook returned to Mia's room and immediately began to wonder what was on Mia's mind. "Hey, girl, you look a million miles away. What are you thinking about?"

"Nothing really. Nothing of any importance anyway. Are we ready to go for a little walk down the hall?"

"Yes, Mia, lets show these folks you can get around, so they'll let you go home."

Mia eased her way out of bed and used the crutches to stabilize herself on one leg. She comfortably tucked the padded part of the crutches under her arms and headed out of the hospital room door. She paused once she was in the hall. She looked to the left and then to the right and decided to head to the left.

"Why do you want to walk this way, Mia? Don't you think we should head towards the nurses desk?"

"No, this will be fine. We are just going to walk to that sign down there and turn around." Mia wanted to look at the sign to determine if she was near the wing of the hospital that she thought she was. Sure enough, the sign at the end of the hall pointed to the Pediatric ICU wing, the very place where her little boy had died.

"Mia, this is far enough, let's go back now. Come on." Brook gently placed her hands on Mia's shoulders and helped her turn in the direction of her room. Brook knew all to well the painful memories that were associated with that area of the hospital, and it wasn't what she wanted Mia to concentrate on. She wanted Mia's focus to be on healing, getting better for herself and for her beautiful little girl.

Once they returned to the room and Mia had gotten settled back into bed, she decided to share with Brook what she'd learned the night of the accident. "Brook, he has another son. David has a toddler aged son with the girl from the picture Tameka gave me."

"Wait a minute…what? Are you sure? How do you know this?"

"The night of the accident, I was looking at a photo of David with his son when I lost control of the car. The boy looks just like David. They looked so happy together. We lost our son, and David went out and tried to replace him with another boy. How could I be so stupid as to think that David and I might somehow be able to work things out? The truth is he stopped loving me a long time ago. This marriage has been over for a while now, and this was just confirmation."

"Oh, Mia, I'm so sorry. I can't imagine what must have been going through your mind when you found out. I mean…hell; I don't even know what to say. This is all so unbelievable."

"Believe it, baby. This is really my situation. And here I was thinking that this sort of thing only happened to the dumb blonde in those Lifetime movies. Well, who's the dumb blonde now?"

"Mia, you are a lot of things, but dumb isn't one of them. What he has done is disgraceful. David is certainly not the man I thought he was. And I don't care how many kids he has, he will never be able to replace your beautiful son."

"You're right. My baby is irreplaceable. Anyway, girl, you've been here long enough. You had better get home and take care of your own babies. They are not used to you being away from home so much during the week."

"Trust me; my rug rats are just fine. They did tell me to give Auntie Mia a big hug and a kiss. So this is from them." Brook leaned over and planted a kiss on Mia's forehead and gave her a gentle squeeze before preparing to leave. Before she could gather all of her things, the door swung open and there stood Adam.

"Hello ladies. How are we this evening?"

"We are fine." Brook chuckled. "But I am going to leave now. Mia, I'll see you tomorrow. If you need anything before then, just call. Adam, take care of our girl."

"You know I will."

As Brook made her departure, Adam made his way to Mia's bedside. He gently leaned over and kissed her on the cheek. "How are you this evening? Did you get up and walk today?"

"Yes sir, I did. I walked to the end of the hallway and back."

"Good for you. For your efforts, I shall reward you with these tulips."

"Adam, you have to stop bringing me flowers every day. It's starting to look like a florist up in here."

"My friend, you should always be surrounded by beautiful things."

"Well thank you, but…"

"But what, Mia?"

"But I don't want you doing all of this, the flowers, the nights on that couch, out of feelings of guilt. The accident was not your fault. You were simply providing the information that you were being paid to gather."

"Do you feel better having said that mess? I'm not here out of guilt; I'm here because I want to be. I want to be by your bedside every night. I want to be someone you can talk to, confide in. I want to be the one bringing you flowers. Mia, you are an amazing woman, and I feel privileged to be around you."

Mia was speechless. The last year or so with David had left her feeling so unloved, unworthy of anyone's adoration. But here was Adam, willing and able to give her everything she'd been missing at home.

The next morning, she awoke to see Adam laying out a small buffet of breakfast foods and juices on top of the small dresser. He turner to see her pulling herself up in bed and winked at her playfully.

"Good morning, sunshine."

"Good morning yourself, what's going on here?"

"I figured you had to be tired of this gross hospital food by now. So, I got us some real breakfast. Do you want to eat in bed or sit up in the chair?"

"How about I sit on that little couch next to you?"

"Perfect."

Adam helped Mia out of bed and to the couch. He prepared her food and placed it on the hospital tray. Once she was settled, he prepared his food, sat beside Mia and chowed down. Just as they had finished their meal and he clearing everything away, the doctor stepped into the room.

"So how is the patient this morning?"

"I'm feeling much better, thank you."

"Glad to hear it. All of your tests have come back normal, and you seem to be getting around a bit better. As you know, it will be a slow road to a full recovery, but I think you're good to go home today."

"Oh, that is great news." Mia squealed.

"Will there be someone available to help you around the house and drive you to all of your follow-up appointments?"

"Absolutely, I've got a great support system."

"Wonderful. I'll go ahead and sign your release papers. The nurse will come in shortly with any additional home instructions, and then you are free to go."

"Thank you so much, doctor," she sang with great appreciation.

As they rolled Mia from her room, she asked if they would mind taking a small detour. The nurse, as well as Adam looked a bit confused but went along with Mia's request. She had them roll her down to Pediatric ICU before heading for the hospital exit. As they made their way down the hall and around the corner, Mia explained to Adam her connection with that wing of the hospital. He could feel the pain that still stirred deeply inside of Mia as she spoke of her late son.

They approached the entrance to the unit and Mia was struck by who she saw. There stood David and the woman from the picture speaking with a physician. Adam motioned for the nurse to stop pushing Mia's wheelchair. They stood there a moment and watched as the visibly shaken couple spoke with the doctor. The woman began to cry and David took her in his arms to comfort her. Instantly tears began to form in Mia's eyes. David turned his head and his eyes met Mia's.

# CHAPTER TWENTY-FIVE

Mia had been home for a few days and was thrilled to be with her daughter again. Little Miss Kaylie had appointed herself *head nurse*. She had been all over Mia ever since she walked in the door three days ago. Mia thought it was so sweet the way Kaylie tried to do everything from prepare her a sandwich to help her get dressed. But Mia had to admit that she was pleased with being alone for a while today. Her mom had taken Kaylie to school and was then running several errands. Now Mia felt safe to deal with some of her emotions.

After retrieving her IPOD and journal, Mia laid back on her chaise and prepared herself to write out her feelings. But when she hit play on the IPOD, Billi Holiday began to sing *Good Morning Heartache*. Mia instantly burst into tears. She cried so mournfully. She cried for the death of her marriage. She cried for the death of the love that David had once felt for her. She cried for the love inside of her that was being suffocated. The love was slowly loosing the ability to breathe the kind of air necessary to keep it alive.

The journal had fallen to the side, and Mia allowed herself to get caught up in the music. She had always believed that there was a song for every situation in life and right now, her theory was proving itself true. Mia was singing along with Anita Baker and declaring the foolishness of *Fairytales* when she jumped at the sound of the front door slamming shut. She grabbed a tissue to dry her eyes and prepared herself to see her mom walk around the corner. But to her surprise, it was David dragging his sorry ass in the room.

"What are you doing here, David?"

"I thought we needed to talk. I owe you an explanation."

"You think?" Mia retorted sarcastically.

David moved across the room slowly and took a seat on the couch directly across from Mia. He didn't speak for what seemed like an eternity. He ran his hands over his head and sighed deeply and continued to sit silently. Mia began to wonder if he would ever find the courage to speak the words that he should have spoken years ago.

"What's wrong, David? Cat got your tongue?"

"I'm sorry, Mia. I'm so very sorry. You don't deserve the foul treatment that I've been giving you. I foolishly thought that if I acted like an ass it would lessen the pain you would feel when I came clean about what's been going on."

"Yes David, that was a very foolish thought. How about you tell me now what has been going on?"

"The lady you saw me with the other day, well, we have a child together. His name is Scottie, and he's twenty-one months old. He's sick." David's voice cracked as he unsuccessfully tried to choke back tears.

"What's wrong with him?"

"Sickle Cell."

"I'm sorry to hear that."

"I just hate to see him in such pain. After what we went through, I never expected that I'd have to deal with it again. I thought that this would be different, you know, a second chance to be a father to my son. My healthy son."

"So you were trying to replace our baby? Unbelievable. Un-freaking-believable!"

"No Mia, I wasn't trying to replace him, it just happened. I couldn't have predicted that when Willow got pregnant that she would have our son. I mean, you know, it was a fifty-fifty shot. But I can't lie and say that I wasn't thrilled when the ultrasound revealed the baby's gender."

"How long have you been with Willow?"

"I'm not really with her. We are very good friends. She wanted a baby and asked me to help her out."

"You helped her out? No idiot! Loaning her money, giving her a ride somewhere, that's how you help out. You, as a married man, don't lay down with a woman and purposefully knock her up as a way of helping out." Mia could hardly contain her anger.

David got up and began to pace around the room. He knew that this would be a difficult conversation, and well, he was right. It was never his intention to hurt Mia, he'd just gotten caught up in so much and didn't know how to explain any of it to his wife.

"So tell me, David, when you decided to start an affair with Zoe right after our son's death, were you just helping her out as well?"

David looked like a deer caught in headlights. "What...I mean who is Zoe?" he stuttered. He wasn't prepared to spill the beans on all of his extra marital activities.

"Are you really going to do this?"

"Mia, I don't know what you want me to say."

"I want you to tell the truth. Don't you think you owe me that?"

David plopped back down on the couch. "Yes, I did become involved with Zoe shortly after the death. I know that I should have turned to you instead, but Zoe was a real comfort to me. She helped me deal with my grief. She loved me through it."

Mia felt sick. "And who was supposed to love *me* through it, David? What was I supposed to do while you were turning to other women and away from me?" She cried mournfully.

"Mia, I'm sorry. Baby, please don't cry, I hate to see you cry."

"Shut up. Don't pretend to give a damn about me now."

"I'm not pretending, I do still care about you. I still love you. I've done some stupid things and been a foolish man, but I never stopped loving you."

"Your actions say that you stopped loving me a long time ago. Let's not pretend otherwise. All I want to know now is if there are any other secrets that I need to know about?"

David looked at Mia intently as if he were trying to decide if there was more to share. Then he turned from her stare "No, there are no more secrets."

"So, how do you want to handle the divorce? Do you want to sell the house and split the proceeds or what? Please keep in mind that I want this as painless as it can possibly be for Kaylie."

"Look Mia, I'm just going through some things right now, but if you can give me a little time…"

"I've given you more time than you deserve. Not to mention the fact that you now have another baby mama. You say there are no more secrets, but I can't believe a word that comes out of your mouth."

"Baby, there are no more secrets."

"Okay, then tell me about this new found friendship of yours with Wayne?"

The expression on David's face was priceless, and it told Mia that there were absolutely more secrets. "Forget it David, how do you want to handle the divorce?"

David stood to his feet, stuffed his hands in his pockets, and cleared his throat. "This is the only home Kaylie has known, and I want to keep it that way. Keep the house, and I promise to be generous with our final settlement, whatever it may be."

"Well, I appreciate that. When can I expect you to come and move your belongings?"

"Damn, Mia, can I have a minute?"

"Only a minute, David, and then I want everything to move quickly. I need to move on with my life, just as you have."

"Okay, okay, it won't be long. By the way, I was sorry to hear about your accident, and I apologize for not making it to see you in the hospital. I assume you'll make a full recovery."

"Thanks to God, yes I will. Now I think it's time for you to go, David."

"Fine, I'll call before I return for my things." David grabbed his keys and headed out the door. He didn't bother to look back at what he was leaving behind.

# CHAPTER TWENTY-SIX

It had been a few weeks since Tameka had attempted to communicate with Wayne about his life and the aspects of it that he chose to keep away from her. Instead of focusing on him, she had decided to throw herself into her work. Yes, she worked for a small, local cable station, but she wanted to be a stand out. She absolutely wanted to be a big fish in this tiny pond. And all of her hard work paid off. She was recently given the opportunity to produce the highest ranking show for the station. Tameka was blown away by the praise and accolades that she received for the show. It was such a satisfying feeling; it made her want more.

Tameka was at her desk working through the upcoming stories when her phone rang. She was both surprised and pissed to find Mia on the other end. "Mia, what could you possibly want, and why are you bothering me at work?"

"Tameka, I'm sorry for interrupting your day. I know that you're busy, but I really wanted to talk with you about Wayne and David."

"Look, Mia, I'm trying hard to refocus my energy away from them. My job is my priority now. I can't be bothered with what those two are doing."

"Are you sure about that? This is someone that you are living with, sleeping with, trying to make a life with. Isn't it in your best interest to know what is going on in his life?"

"Like I said, my concentration is on my job, and that's where I'm going to keep it. Goodbye." Tameka hung up the phone and returned to the task at hand.

A few hours later, Tameka entered her home with an evening of relaxation in mind. She was pleased to see that Wayne had beaten her home. They could enjoy a simple meal, maybe take-out, and watch a movie in bed or something. But once she saw Wayne's face, it was obvious that those plans were out the window.

"Hi honey, what's wrong, why do you look so stressed?" Tameka inquired.

"I have some news to share with you," Wayne announced as he paced the floor.

"Okay, I'm listening."

"I'm not sure if you are aware, but David and I have become pretty good friends. Well, he has a son, Scottie, who is quite ill. The baby suffers from Sickle Cell."

Tameka plopped down in a chair with her mouth gaped open. She couldn't help but wonder if Mia knew about her husband's sick love child. She shook her head, trying to clear the fog so that she could continue to hear clearly what Wayne was saying.

"There is a relatively new procedure where they can do a bone marrow transplant and possibly cure, or should I say dramatically improve Scottie's life with this debilitating disease. I happen to be a perfect match."

"What?"

"I'm a match."

"I heard your ass, but I can't understand why you give a damn if you're a match."

"David is a good friend, Tameka. He needs me now. This could mean life or death for his son."

"When did y'all get to be such good friends that you're

willing to risk your life for his son? Let David donate the damn bone marrow."

"Don't you think that if he or the boy's mother could, they would?"

"Then please, please, Wayne, help me to understand the basis of this friendship? I mean, hell, I got friends that I've had for years, but I'm not trying to cough up body parts for them."

"I'm not like you, Tameka, and I think we all know that. While you were away, I met David through a mutual business partner, and we just became friends. Why is the concept of self-sacrifice for the good of another so hard for you to comprehend?"

"No, this gay ass friendship is what's hard for me to understand."

Wayne found himself stepping to Tameka with an anger he'd never experienced. Before he realized it, he had his hand around her neck, threatening her life. "Bitch, if you ever call me gay again I will snap your damn neck. Do you hear me?" He growled as he pushed her away.

"A hit dog will holler; won't he, Wayne?" Tameka grabbed her purse and headed out the door.

Five in the morning and Tameka found herself sitting in a cheap motel room trying to imagine Wayne's life while she was away in prison. He was always so strong for her, supportive of her. But he must have been far more lonely than she ever imagined. Working every day, visiting her monthly and always coming home to an empty house. Could he have possibly been desperate enough to turn to another man? Then she reasoned "hell no". There are fifty million single women in Atlanta ready to throw themselves at a handsome, employed man. So with that in mind, Tameka realized that she was back at square one. What was the friendship between Wayne and David all about? It was time to put her investigative hat back on.

After calling out of work, Tameka drove home to what she hoped would be an empty house. She wasn't in the mood for another confrontation with Wayne. Her only desire was to get a good, hot shower and contemplate her next move. Thankfully, Wayne was not home.

After making a few phone calls and confirming that both Wayne and David were at their respective jobs, Tameka decided that it was time to reconnect with Mia. She carefully dialed the number and waited for Mia to pick up.

"Hello?"

"Mia, this is Tameka…"

"This is not Mia. It's Brook, and what the hell are you doing calling here?"

"Aw hell, I'm getting so sick of you that I don't even know what to do with myself. For your information, I'm returning Mia's call. Would you please put her on the line?"

"I can't imagine that Mia would have called you for anything. I thought I asked you nicely to stay away from her."

"You know what Brook…" Tameka began to yell. But before she could finish, she heard a different voice on the line.

"Tameka, it's me, Mia."

"Mia, I knew it was a mistake calling you. Forget I dialed your number."

"No, Tameka, please don't hang up. Something had to have happened for you to call."

"Yeah, I need to know how much you know about David, his child, and Wayne?"

"Look, Tameka, there seems to be so much that we need to sort out. Why don't you just come over here so we can talk and try to get to the bottom of this mess?"

"Mia, this is already a difficult day for me. I don't need your pit bull, Brook, over there barking at me."

"I promise there won't be any barking, yelling, or anything else. I assume you know the address."

"Yes, I've got it. But I'm warning you, I won't be responsible if Brook jumps her ass in my face."

"She won't. Just come on over."

It wasn't long before Tameka was pulling up and parking in front of Mia's house. To say she was surprised to see Mia in her current physical condition would be an understatement.

"What the hell happened to you?"

Mia invited Tameka to come in and take a seat. She proceeded to fill Tameka in on what had happened and about the discovery of David's son. Mia waited for a look of shock to cross Tameka's face, but instead, she was the one surprised by the lack of any kind of reaction from Tameka.

"I take it you know about the little boy?" Mia quizzed.

"Yes, I do. Is there anything else that you know about the child?"

"Just that he's sick. Bless him; he suffers from Sickle Cell Anemia."

"Anything else?"

"No, Tameka. Now stop with the Spanish Inquisition and tell me what you know."

Before Tameka began to speak, Brook sashayed her narrow tail in the room and sat directly across from Tameka.

Tameka rolled her eyes and began to share what she had been told by Wayne. "There is a possibility that the child can be cured with a bone marrow transplant. Guess who their perfect match is…Wayne."

"What?" Mia exclaimed. "That is so random, how would they have even known to test him? How close are they?"

"That's what I asked, but all I got was choked out. Behavior that is very out of character for Wayne. He got so upset that I didn't even stay there last night. I've tried asking him about his connection with David, but he immediately shuts down. He finally did tell me that they met through a work thing and just became friends. But it is definitely a touchy subject for him," Tameka explained.

"David hasn't even been staying here. He came by long enough to tell me about his son and for me to get clarity about our inevitable divorce. So what's the next step? Where do we go from here?"

"Mia, you don't need her to help you sort this out." Brook interjected. "You have Adam. He's a professional and will be able to gather more information than this one ever could," she blurted as she waved her hand in Tameka's direction.

"Brook, I'm just a little sick of your ass. I haven't had anything to say to you, do with you, nor do I have a desire to interact with you. Now if you keep screwing with me, I'm going to show you what I'm really capable of. I have done my time, paid my debt to society and all that shit. Now you are going to step away and leave me the hell alone." Tameka spewed with more venom than any snake ever could.

"Brook, I know you are concerned for me, and yes, Adam is a professional. However, Tameka was the first to come to me with any information. This is a good opportunity for us to share information and find out what is going on," Mia pleaded.

"Fine, do what you feel you need to do, Mia. But don't say that I didn't warn you. You know she's evil, and I know that nothing good will come of this little alliance. Just promise me you'll watch your back. Trust, she'll stab you in the back just like she did me. I just hope she doesn't kill anyone that you love." Brook grabbed her purse and stormed out of the door.

Mia was torn. She wanted to show her devotion to her friendship with Brook but had to get information on David by any means necessary. Tameka had already decided to go along with the plan to work with Mia. She could really use the help of a detective; one person could only do so much. As for Brook, Tameka had already gotten comfortable with the decision to show her what evil really looked like.

# CHAPTER TWENTY-SEVEN

Brook drove home with a heavy heart and tears rolling down her cheeks. She loved Mia with every fiber of her being, but she wasn't sure that the feelings were mutual anymore. Mia was like a sister to Brook. They had been close since college and the friendship had grown stronger over the years. Mia was a real rock for Brook after the death of her parents and after Tameka caused the death of her unborn child. But now, it felt as if Mia was turning her back on all that Tameka had put Brook through. How could Mia trust Tameka for anything?

The garage door came down behind Brook, and she sat in the car to gather herself before going in the house. She took a few deep breathes, opened the car door and stepped out. As soon as she entered the house, the children ran in the room and wrapped themselves around her legs. With this kind of love, how could she not find a way to smile? Brook hugged and kissed on her babies and asked about their day. They filled her in on every second of all that had transpired in their little lives that day. Everything for them seemed so very dramatic. It was hard to maintain a straight face while they talked about the tragedy of broken toys.

Eric had a late business dinner and Brook was going crazy

waiting for his arrival. Eric was her sounding board. As much as Eric loved Brook, he had no problem telling her when she was wrong, overreacting, or just otherwise tripping. She didn't feel like any of that applied in this case. Brook was seriously wounded by the path that Mia had opted to take in order to gain information on her cheating husband.

By the time Eric made it home, Brook had drifted off to sleep. He was trying his best to be quiet and not disturb his sleeping wife. He went into the bathroom, closed the door and took a quick shower to wash away the stresses of the day. He returned to the bedroom, ready to fall asleep. But when he saw Brook lying there in the glow of the television, the thought of sleep went right out of his head. Eric climbed into bed, leaned over and gently kissed his wife. The touch of his lips and hands on her body immediately caused Brook to awaken.

Without ever opening her eyes, she wrapped her arms around Eric and began to kiss him passionately. Eric took his time caressing Brook's body. In one smooth motion, he had her gown off and tossed to the floor. He kissed her neck and slowly made his way to her breasts. He licked and sucked her nipples to a state of erection, first one and then the other. Brook moaned with pleasure. He moved further down her body, pausing at her navel. Who knew that that was an erogenous zone? Brook certainly didn't before Eric came into her life. His tongue continued its journey down and he teased her as he kissed her inner thighs and lightly fondled her clitoris with his fingers. Just when she thought he would kiss her there, he slid back up and kissed her on the mouth. Brook felt that she might explode with anticipation. But before he could search out her wetness with his tongue, she decided to take charge and rolled over on top of her man. It was her turn to kiss down his body until she came upon the fullness of his excitement. But Brook wasn't in the mood to tease; she wanted him and took his full erection into her mouth. Slowly, she moved her head up and down, taking him in inch by inch. Her hands worked in conjunction with her mouth until she felt that Eric was about to cum. Just before his release, she came up, straddled him and welcomed him in. She moved her hips back and forth, up and down and around and around until her juices flowed all over him. Eric's body jerked and he moaned with unbridled pleasure as his body released its strength into the love of his life.

Morning came and sunlight crept through the windows gently encouraging Brook and Eric to ease into a new day. Brook turned over and rested her head on Eric's chest. As they lay there, Eric began to run his fingers through Brook's hair. It was one of his favorite things to do. "Babe, are you okay?" he asked softly. "I get the feeling that something is bothering you."

"Just thinking about everything that's going on with Mia. Can't seem to get passed how she's allowing Tameka access to her life."

"What do you mean access? How much is Tameka involved in Mia's affairs?"

"Apparently, David has a young son with another woman. This child has Sickle Cell Anemia, and a bone marrow transplant could be a possible cure for him. Now here's the kicker, guess who the donor is going to be? None other than Wayne."

"What the hell!" Eric was in a complete state of shock. "I can't believe what I'm hearing. It's like I never knew David at all. Another child…wow."

"Yes. Needless to say, Mia is devastated."

"Brook, what I don't understand is why or how Wayne came to be a donor for David's child?"

"Sweetie, that's where Tameka comes in. Mia actually had Tameka over to her house yesterday to see if she had or could get any information about the connection between David and Wayne. No one understands how these two got to be so tight. And even though Mia has Adam, she feels that Tameka can gather information that Adam either can't or will take too long to uncover. But I have to be honest, I feel like Mia is betraying me by having anything to do with Tameka. She knows what that crazy ass Tameka put us though."

"Brook, this is all pretty deep stuff. I think that we both know that Mia would never betray you. But this is more than she has ever had to deal with. I think that if the tables were turned, we'd take pretty desperate measures to gain information as well. Mia would never intentionally hurt you. As hard as it is, I think that you need to throw your support behind your friend. But, stay the hell away from Tameka. I want you as far away from that deranged creature as possible. Understand?"

"Yes dear, I hear you. You can find comfort in the fact that I want nothing to do with that heffa. I just don't want her causing problems. Mia's life is complicated enough without having to worry about what havoc Tameka will reek upon it."

"Mia is just doing what she feels she has to right now. But you, you steer clear of Tameka, no matter what," Eric demanded.

"Yeah baby, I hear you, I understand and I shall keep a safe distance from her. I promise."

# CHAPTER TWENTY-EIGHT

It had been several days since Tameka's visit to Mia's house. Mia was feeling very torn between her need for the information that Tameka could potentially supply and her loyalty to Brook. Brook had not said anything to Mia about the situation, but she could sense that something was off with Brook. She could feel the distance between them. It was as if Brook was slowly stepping back, creating new boundaries for them to work within. Mia had tried discussing Tameka's temporary roll in her life, but Brook simply didn't want to partake in that conversation.

Mia was slowly moving about the house making sure that everything was in its place. She wanted her abode as neat and clean as possible. Adam was coming over and even though he'd seen her home before, she still had this unexplained desire for him to see her and all that surrounded her in the best possible light. Once Mia determined that everything was perfect, or at least perfect enough, she hobbled off to the shower. As the hot water ran over her body, Mia couldn't help but laugh at herself. She knew darn well why her desires were for Adam to see her in a positive light. Brook saw this coming a mile away and had giggled her knowledge to Mia. It was all quit simple...she *really* liked Adam.

This was all so new to Mia. Nothing in her life was as she had planed it to be. Mia never imagined that she'd have a cheating husband, a broken body, an open dialog happening with Tameka, or a crush on her private investigator. Hell, she never thought she'd have a need for a private investigator. But one thing that Mia did know was that she was still a married woman, and she had no plans on becoming an adulterer. She couldn't help how David chose to live his life, but she did have full control of herself. Mia knew that she was strong enough to stay true to herself and her beliefs. Besides, she was the one with the crush; no one ever said that the feelings were mutual.

Mia checked herself in the mirror and was pleased with the reflection that looked back at her. Just as she turned to walk away, the doorbell rang. "Hi Adam, come on in." Adam entered the house and greeted Mia with a warm embrace. "Can I get you anything, Adam?"

"No, thank you. I'm good. How have you been doing?" he asked as he took a seat across from Mia in the family room.

"Improving every day. So tell me, have you found any new information? I'm hoping that between you and Tameka, I can pull all of this mess together and find out all that there is to know about David and his other life."

"What do you mean between me and Tameka? What does she have to do with any of this?"

"Well, you know that she has shared some information with me. Remember, David and her boyfriend, Wayne, are really good friends now. We're trying to understand their connection."

"Mia, it's my understanding that this Tameka chick is nothing but trouble. She did some pretty awful things to Brook, correct?"

"Yes, but…" Before Mia could finish her response, Adam began to talk again.

"But nothing, Mia. You have enough going on in your life without inviting additional problems."

"I'm not inviting problems, Adam. I'm trying to get answers."

"But at what cost, Mia?" How does Brook feel about this sharing of information between you and Tameka? Are you going to tell me that she's cool with it?"

"No, but when it's all over, she'll understand. Besides, Wayne is sharing things with Tameka that I would not have otherwise found out about."

"Like what Mia, the fact that Wayne is donating bone marrow to try and save David's kid? Is that the kind of information you're talking about?"

"Well, how was I supposed to know that you would find that out?"

"By trusting me to do my job and trusting me to have your best interest at heart, Mia."

"I do trust you Adam. You have to understand that this is all new to me. I can't stand feeling like the stupid, naive wife that couldn't handle her marriage or keep her husband happy. I've got to know all that I can about David and his life now. I have to take back control of this situation. If that means dealing with Tameka, then so be it." Mia ranted with tears in her eyes.

Adam stood up and walked over to Mia. He cautiously sat down beside her and took her hand. "Mia, when I look at you, I see an intelligent, beautiful, strong woman that is handling her business in spite of the situation she's been put in. David's the fool in all of this, not you."

Adam continued to hold Mia's hand for a moment, and then he found himself leaning in to kiss her. Without thinking, Mia returned his kiss, and it slowly escalated from a kind, gentle smooch to one of lustful passion. Mia could feel her body temperature rise, and in her head, she heard herself saying, 'Are you really letting this happen?' Slowly, Mia pulled away. Was it what she wanted to do? No, but she knew it was the right thing to do.

"I'm sorry; I shouldn't have done that." Adam apologized.

"Please, don't apologize. That was both of us, not just you. But, Adam, I can't let that happen again."

"I understand. How about we get back to business," Adam suggested, but business was the last thing on his mind. He'd found himself unbelievably attracted to Mia the first time he laid eyes on her. He knew that it was inappropriate. He was hired to help her, not take advantage or seduce her in her emotionally weakened state. As hard as it was, he regained focus and got back to work.

"I'm currently waiting for a background check to come back on the woman that David is involved with. Something tells me that there is a connection between the woman and Wayne as well. This threesome is very suspicious. I should have more on that within the next twenty-four to forty-eight hours." Adam was trying his best to sound stern and professional, not like a man in heat.

"I wonder what in the world could it be that draws the three of them together. This is all such a mess. I wonder if I should continue to pursue it. I mean, look at me. I'm actually working with Tameka, of all people, and jeopardizing my friendship with Brook. Maybe I should just file the divorce papers and go to court with what I have."

"Do you mean that?" Adam questioned.

"Part of me does, but the bigger part of me wants to know every little secret detail of David's life. I think I deserve to know."

"Then, Mia, I will find everything out for you. I don't need any help, so you may want to consider dropping Tameka from your spy detail."

"Well, I will certainly take that under advisement," Mia chuckled.

"There's that beautiful smile," Adam quipped. "I'm sorry, I shouldn't have said that. Umm…that's all I have for now. I'll call you as soon as the other information comes in." Adam stood to his feet in preparation to leave.

"Please don't apologize. I don't want us to be uncomfortable with one another. You've become important to me, and I don't want this to become a strained relationship."

"Don't worry, Mia, we're good."

Mia escorted Adam to the door. They stood there for an awkward second, and then she reached to hug him. He returned her embrace and they found themselves lingering just a little too long. Slowly he pulled away and walked to his car. As Adam drove away from the house, every part of Mia wanted to scream for him to come back.

# CHAPTER TWENTY-NINE

It had been a busy couple of days for Tameka; work really had her stretched thin. They were giving her more responsibility than she'd ever imagined they would. Tameka was not complaining though, she was actually very pleased with her employer's growing faith in her. Her only regret was that she hadn't had time to put her latest scheme into action. No, it had nothing to do with Wayne. It was much more personal than that.

Tameka had tried and tried to forget about her last encounter with Brook. She'd poured herself into her work, made nice with Wayne, and struggled to occupy her mind with any and everything except Brook. Unfortunately, it always came back to Brook Mansfield-Banks and her holier-than-thou attitude. How dare she sit in such harsh judgment of others? Had nothing Tameka accomplished since her release made a difference to Brook? How could she not see how hard Tameka was working to move her life in a more positive direction? Just who the hell did Brook think she was? Tameka had decided that lessons would have to be taught. Then, maybe Brook would back off.

It was the start of a new day, and Tameka watched the rising of the sun from the comfort of the driver's seat in her car. She had quietly left home at 5:30a.m. and made her way across town. She had used her connections at the station to obtain the security code and let herself into the gated community. Even in the darkness, she could see how magnificent the homes were. Tameka couldn't understand how some folks were blessed to live so well while others struggled to find their next meal. It simply wasn't fair. Especially when half of the folks up in this subdivision didn't deserve to live the good life.

Just when she was beginning to grow impatient, Tameka saw the garage door go up. Brook's car backed out and began its decent down the long, tree-lined driveway. Tameka slumped down in the car seat so that she wouldn't be noticed. After Brook had gotten a good three car lengths ahead of her, Tameka pulled off and began to follow her. Tameka managed to go unnoticed for the entire trip to school. She sat back and watched as Brook escorted her kids into the building. She snapped a couple of pictures so that she could become more familiar with the children. Tameka had no intention of wasting her time with the wrong kids. She glanced at her watch and decided that she'd better make haste. Tameka did not want to be late for work.

By lunch time, Tameka had finished with the bulk of her work for the day. It was time to put part two of her plan into action.

"Thank you for calling Birdwell Academy. How may I help you?"

"Hello, my name is Monica Greer, investigative reporter for Local Network News. I am a friend of Mrs. Brook Mansfield-Banks, and she suggested I give you all a call."

"Oh yes, the Banks family are great friends of the school. What can we help you with?"

"I'm doing a story on education, more specifically, public vs. private education. I would love to examine one of your first grade classes for my comparison piece. Do you think that would be possible?"

"Well Ms. Greer, we do pride ourselves on delivering the highest quality education to our children. When would you like to come in for this observation?"

"I know its short notice, but this afternoon if possible. I could be there in thirty minutes."

"Oh, that soon. May I please place you on hold for a moment just to confirm with our principal that it will be okay?"

"Of course." Tameka couldn't help but grin at the fact that she'd gotten this far. All you have to do is mention television and people lose it. Everybody wants their fifteen minutes of fame. And just as Tameka expected, the young woman returned to the phone with good news.

"Ms. Greer, our principal, Ms. Howard says she'd be honored to have you come out and observe one of our classes. What time should we expect you?"

"Wonderful! I will be there by 1:30 pm."

"Alright, we'll see you then. Goodbye."

"Bye-bye." Tameka hung up the phone and began to giggle like a little school girl. She grabbed her bag and headed out of the door. Twenty minutes later, she was parking her car, grabbing her camera bag, and heading into the Birdwell Academy.

Tameka met with the principal and some of the other staff. They gave her a brief tour of the facility and some background information on how the school was established. It wasn't long before they made it to one of the first grade classes. Lucky for Tameka, it happen to be the one that Brook's baby girl was in.

Tameka was introduced to the class as Ms. Greer. All of the kids were so excited about being on television. Each child must have asked Tameka no less than five questions. They were fascinated by the camera. Once the teacher calmed them all back down, Tameka continued to tape them, even though there was no film in the camera, it was just for show. She moved around the room as the teacher continued with the day's lesson. Tameka hung out a little longer, asked the kids their names, and found out what their recess time was. She had all the information she'd come for. As she packed up to leave and the children started to say their goodbyes, Tameka leaned in and whispered in Brook's daughter's ear, "Make sure you tell your mommy that I said hi." The little girl was all too happy to do as she was told.

# CHAPTER THIRTY

By the time Brook made it in from the office, the housekeeper had picked the kids up from school, fed them, and was helping with homework. She eased into the family room just in time to hear her daughter reading a story. It was such a sweet sound. Brook was so proud of her children. They were well-rounded, intelligent, respectful little people that excelled at their school work and extra-curricular activities. When she looked at them, she saw all that was right with the world. If only her parents had lived to see them.

"Mommy, you're home." Kristen took off running and flung herself into her mom's arms.

"Yes, my little angel, Mommy is home." Brook giggled in between the kisses that she planted all over the face of her baby.

"Get back over here and finish the story," Brook's son demanded. Michael was unfazed by Brook's arrival. He wanted his story, and that's all that mattered to him at the time.

"Be quiet! Can't you see Mommy is here?"

"But you promised to read the whole book. You're not done yet."

"Okay guys," Brook chimed in. "How about I join you all on the sofa, and we can all hear the rest of the story?"

"Great, come on Mom," her daughter exclaimed as she pulled Brook by the hand.

Brook joined everyone in the family room, plopped down on the floor next to her son, and enjoyed the remainder of a story about a wicked witch and seven little people. Because of who was reading it, it was the absolute best book that anyone had ever read. Before the tale could be completed, the little boy was fast asleep in his mom's lap. Brook gently pulled her son into her arms, stood to her feet, and carried the sleeping tot to his room. Of course she was followed closely by Kristen.

"Mommy, are you going to put me to bed next?"

"Yes, angel."

"Will you lay down with me until I fall asleep?"

"Of course I will," Brook responded as she carefully laid her son in his bed, kissed his forehead and eased out of the room.

"Alright angel, it's your turn. Let's go to bed." Brook led her daughter to her room, tucked her in, and got comfortable on top of the covers beside her. "Mommy loves you so very much, angel."

"I love you too, Mommy." And right before the sleepy little girl could drift off, she decided to share a little information. "Oh Mommy, the nice lady at school today told me to tell you hello."

"What lady, baby?'

"The lady who was holding the camera. She told me to tell you hello."

"What kind of camera did she have, honey?"

"The kind that sat on her shoulder. She said we would be on TV."

Brook sat straight up in the bed. Her mind was flying, who in the world did she know that would be taping the children? "Damn it, Tameka!" Brook exclaimed.

"Mommy, you cursed."

"Oh baby, Mommy is sorry. I didn't mean to curse. Shame on me! I won't do it again."

"Are you mad at me for talking to the lady? She was really nice, and the teacher said it was okay to talk to her."

"Baby, Mommy is not mad or upset with you. I love you, and I didn't mean to curse. Do you forgive me?"

"Yes, I forgive you, but don't do it again."

"I won't," Brook chuckled. As upset as she was at the possibility of Tameka being around her child, her daughters chastising her was too funny. Brook couldn't help herself; she had to laugh.

It wasn't long before both kids were fast asleep and Brook was standing under a hot shower contemplating the possibility of Tameka actually having balls enough to visit her child's classroom. But if she had, how did she get past the principal and in the good graces of the classroom teacher? The more she thought about it, the more she started to believe that it couldn't be Tameka. The school was too protective of their students to let someone as unstable as Tameka Williams slither among them.

Brook dressed for bed, climbed in between the sheets, and clicked on the television. Here she was alone again. Business had taken her husband away from her and planted him in LA for a day filled with business meetings. She was grateful that the airline would deliver him back to her tomorrow and was anxious for him to arrive. She hated sleeping alone. After flipping channels for a few minutes, Brook decided that there was nothing on that was worthy of her attention. She flicked the television off, grabbed her husband's pillow, and wrapped herself around it. She thought once more about the whole school thing and decided that she'd talk with the teacher in the morning when she dropped off the kids just to ease her mind. Then she buried her head further into Eric's pillow so that she could smell his scent and drifted off to sleep.

Morning came and Brook jumped up, got herself and the kids ready for their day and headed out the door. The children chatted her up all the way to school. It was almost a little competition as to who would get to talk to her the most. Once the kids were delivered safely to their classrooms, Brook made her way to the principal's office.

"Hi, is Ms. Madison available?" Brook quizzed the secretary.

"Hi, Mrs. Banks. Yes she is; step on in her office."

"Thanks," Brook smiled and moved on to the office. "Hi Mrs. Madison, how are you this morning?"

"I'm great, thanks for asking. What can I do for you this morning, Mrs. Banks?"

"My daughter mentioned that there was a woman here yesterday filming footage in their class. I wanted to ask who this person was and to make sure that it was approved by you."

"Oh yes, it was a young lady named Monica Greer with the local cable news channel. They are doing an investigative report on private vs. public schools in the area and wanted to use our school as a shining example of the benefits of a private education. We're really looking forward to seeing the piece and adding it as part of our recruiting package."

"Oh, okay, I just wanted to make sure that everything was cleared with you and that it was a legitimate thing. You know, you can never be too careful these days?"

"I agree completely, but we checked credentials and all."

"Great, thank you for your time, Mrs. Madison. I hope you have a great day, and I'll see you later."

"Same to you, Mrs. Banks. Good day."

# CHAPTER THIRTY-ONE

Mia had almost completely recovered from her injuries and was now trying to decide just how much longer she would stay away from work. She knew her time was winding down and that she'd have to return within the next week or two. The days of having hubby to fall back on financially were over. She had to jump back in full force and very soon. The bills had to be paid, and she was on her own. But, hell, she wasn't scared; Mia had done it for herself long before David ever came along. The only difference now was that she was Mia plus one, the plus one of course, was her baby girl. But Mia was ready to put on her cape and play super woman. She was confident that she could be all things that she and Kaylie needed. Mia's only concern was getting as much of this divorce crap taken care of as she possibly could before returning to work. She would be racing against the clock.

Mia grabbed her keys and headed out the door. She was first meeting Adam for brunch and was looking forward to hearing about any new developments. But, she was mostly looking forward to just sharing space with the man. True, she was still married and was determined to stay faithful to her vows. But, that didn't mean she couldn't admire a good man or enjoy an innocent meal with him. After brunch, she would head over to Brook's house for a short visit.

As she whipped her car into a parking space, Mia noticed Adam's car parked a couple of spaces over. She was pleased that he beat her there. That meant that he'd probably already gotten seated. Mia jumped out of the car and headed around the corner where she entered Mary Mac's Tea Room, a quaint restaurant that had become part of the fabric of Atlanta. As soon as she crossed the threshold, she spotted Adam. He stood to his feet and greeted her with a gentle kiss to the cheek. As he held the chair for her, Adam couldn't deny that his desire to be closer to her was growing stronger day by day.

"Wow, Mia, you are looking gorgeous. How are you feeling?"

"I'm feeling great and the doctor has given me clearance to return to normal activity. How are you today?"

"I'm really good. I have no complaints, none at all. Have you decided when you're going to return to work?"

"I've been thinking about that a lot today, and I've decided to give myself one more week off. I'm hoping that I'll be able to get David to review the divorce papers so that our attorneys can start fighting over the details. I'm ready to move on."

"Unfortunately, I think that that is going to have to wait. I just found out that the transplant surgery is taking place tomorrow," Adam regretfully stated. He knew that this was not what Mia wanted to hear.

"Wow, well for the baby's sake, I hope it all goes well. But I have to wonder what this means for my daughter. She has been constantly asking for her father. So if he was too distracted to call or visit before, she really doesn't stand a snow ball's chance in hell of seeing him now."

"Does she know anything about her dad having another child?"

"Oh no. Her knowledge of the divorce is more than enough for her little heart to deal with."

"I hear you. Well, I've got a couple of additional photos for you. It's David with the same woman but you know I have not been able to catch them in an intimate type photo. It's always a friendly embrace or them just standing side by side. Of course we know that they are involved, they have a child. But it's weird; they just don't seem like a true couple. There doesn't seem to be any kind of spark between them."

"I don't get that. David has always been a very passionate man. He loves the public displays of affection, so I find it quite odd that he's not all over this woman. It's obviously not out of any kind of respect for me. He spat disrespect in my face a long time ago."

"And that makes him the fool. No one in their right mind would ever disrespect you."

"Thank you," Mia mumbled with a slight smile on her face.

"I say we forget about David for a bit and order some of this delicious food," Adam suggested.

"Now that's the best idea I've heard today."

Before they realized it, two hours had flown by. Mia and Adam thoroughly enjoyed their meal, and then got lost in one another. The conversation flowed and not one word was spoken of David. They chose to share memories of their childhood, feelings of the emotional lows and highs of life, and political views. They covered almost every topic but never tired of the words they shared. It took a lot of strength for each of them to pull away from the table. Adam walked Mia to her car and literally had to force himself to say goodbye without leaning in for a kiss. They drove off in opposite directions despite the fact that they both wanted to continue to share time and space with one another.

"You're running a little late, aren't you girlie?" Brook quizzed as she ushered Mia through the house to the kitchen.

"What can I say? Lunch ran late."

"Did Adam have any additional information about David? Anything that can help push the divorce along?"

"Nothing! In fact, it's the complete opposite. The transplant surgery is happening tomorrow. I can imagine that David is going to be far too distracted to give any attention to divorce papers."

"That's just crazy to me. I mean, I'm glad for the child. It's a blessing that he'll have an opportunity to live a full life without the pain of Sickle Cell, however, I wish I knew the connection that makes Wayne the perfect donor. What in the world pulled Wayne and David so close that they would sacrifice their body parts for one another's child?"

"Damn, Brook, you are full of questions that I would pay good money to have the answers to. I was hoping that Tameka would be able to shed a little light on some of this. Unfortunately, she hasn't been able to provide any more information than Adam has. The pictures that she's taken run along the same lines as the ones Adam has taken. So far, she's been a useless fountain of information. With that being said, I'm sorry Brook."

"Sorry for what?" Brook asked as she poured up a couple of glasses of iced tea.

"I'm sorry for not respecting your feelings more when it came to my dealing with Tameka. I know all too well what she put you through, but I got so caught up in my own issues that I allowed her to slither into our lives again. I never meant to push you away by allowing her into my life."

"Mia, no apologies necessary," Brook lied.

"Girl please, stop playing. We both know how hurt you were by all of this, and we both know that an apology was very necessary. I just hope that you know it was sincere?"

"Yes, I do." Brook grabbed Mia and embraced her with such love and relief. The apology freed her from the doubts she'd begun to have about the strength of their friendship.

The ladies laughed and talked for a while longer before Mia

made note of the time and her need to head back to her side of town. As they approached the front door, Brook remembered the question she'd wanted to ask Mia. "Mia, do you know what station Monica Greer is working for now?"

"What in the world made you ask about her?"

"Apparently, she was at the kid's school the other day doing a piece on public vs. private schools, and the majority of the story took place in my little princess's class. She was all excited to tell me that the news lady told her to tell me hi."

"Brook, you may want to check with the school office because Monica Greer moved out of the Atlanta market a few months ago."

"Are you sure?"

"Sweetie, I'm positive. You know she landed a local entertainment show a little while back. Apparently, that opened other doors for her, and she has moved on to bigger and better things in the Washington DC market."

"Who the hell is creeping around my kid's school?"

The ladies looked at one another and simultaneously blurted, "Tameka."

# CHAPTER THIRTY-TWO

Curiosity was killing Mia. She had resigned herself to staying away from the hospital today. She'd all but convinced herself that what was taking place was none of her concern, none of her business. But the fact of the matter was her husband's child was getting a bone marrow transplant today. Surely the outcome of this surgery would affect her life and the life of her own child. David had already stepped so far back from their home life and their little girl that little Miss Kaylie had almost forgotten what her daddy looked like.

To her own surprise, within the hour, Mia found herself walking through the sliding doors of the hospital. She slowly made her way to the children's ward and located the surgical waiting room. She turned the corner to see David waiting there with the young lady from the pictures. To say he was stunned to see her would be an understatement.

"Mia, what are you doing here?" he questioned as he let go of the woman's hand.

"I'm not sure, David. I don't understand why I felt so compelled to be here. Is there any news yet?"

"No, they just took them back to surgery about thirty

minutes ago. Umm, I guess I should make some type of introduction. Mia, this is…" Mia raised her hand to cut him off.

"I know who she is." Mia looked in the woman's direction. "Sorry that your child is ill, I'm confident he'll come through this just fine."

"Thank you," the woman stammered.

Without saying another word, Mia took a seat and decided to wait it out for a while. To Mia's surprise, Tameka showed up a short time later to check on Wayne and the progress of the surgery. Mia had assumed that Tameka would have been the one to drive Wayne to the hospital and sit lovingly by his side. He had stuck with her through so much, so Mia could not imagine why Tameka wasn't there from start to finish of this process.

"Any news?" Tameka inquired as she took a seat.

"No" was all David could seem to muster.

"Why the attitude?" Tameka spat in David's direction.

Mia politely interjected. "Tameka, now is not the time. Why don't we all just wait quietly and patiently?"

"Whatever," Tameka retorted.

It wasn't a minute later that another young woman came walking into the room carrying three cups of coffee. She walked directly to David and his woman and began to pass them the hot beverages. As she leaned over towards her friends, both Mia and Tameka took notice of her tall, slim build. The woman had legs for days. She had a smooth, dark chocolate complexion with very defined facial features. She would put one in the mind of a young Grace Jones but only softer, more feminine. She took a seat beside David's woman and then to the surprise of Mia and Tameka, she leaned in to the woman for a gentle kiss on the mouth and softly, lovingly asked if there was any news. Mia and Tameka's eyes instantly met as if to ask, "What the hell?"

David immediately became uncomfortable. He was squirming in his seat like a child that had to go potty. The intensity of his facial expression made him look as though he might be in physical pain. Could it be that some part of his deep, dark secret was about to be revealed?

"So, David, aren't you going to introduce us to your lady friends?" Tameka blurted.

"Tameka, I don't think that any introductions are needed or required."

"Well I don't know, David. Seems we're all here out of concern for the patients. We should at least know with whom we share all of this concern," Tameka pushed. This time, Mia said nothing.

"No one invited you here or asked for your concern, Tameka. Now let it go." David demanded.

"I didn't need an invitation. In case you've forgotten, that's my man back there trying to save your kid's life."

"No one has forgotten," interjected the child's mother. I'm Willow and this is my girlfriend Pam. I am also Wayne's little sister. So while you're concerned for your *man*, I'm concerned for my brother and my child."

"Oh hell no," Tameka blurted as she stood to her feet. "I've been with Wayne for years now, and he's never once mentioned a sister."

"Then maybe that speaks to the depths of your relationship. Maybe if you had ever once asked about his family instead of thinking up new ways to get in trouble, you might have known about me. But no, you've never cared about Wayne, only about how he could be there for you."

"Wayne would have told me about any siblings. He told me about his parents when I asked."

"What did he tell you? Let me guess, that they died when we were younger, right?"

"Right." stammered a confused Tameka.

"And did you ask about any other living relatives?" Willow badgered her.

"Well no, I assumed he would tell me if he had any other relatives."

"Then that makes you the ass, Tameka."

"Willow, please." David was pulling on her hand, almost begging her to sit down and shut up.

"No David, I'm tired of keeping secrets for everybody, from everybody. Wayne has dedicated so much time to this idiot, and she has never given so much as a rat's ass about him." Willow continued on her tirade.

"Willow, sit down!" David demanded. "Every damn secret ain't yours to tell. How the hell do you think Wayne would feel about you going off like this? Now sit your ass down and shut up."

Willow did as she was instructed. Needless to say that both Mia and Tameka were stunned and dying inside to know what secrets David was referring to. Mia could hardly wait to share all of this with Adam.

Within the hour, the surgeon emerged from the operating room and advised the parents that the transplant went well and both patients were in recovery. He ushered David and Willow through the double doors so that they could visit with their child.

Adam had been out of town all week and it was killing Mia not to be able to speak with him about all that had transpired. Yes, she could have shared the information over the phone; he had called her every day, but this was something she wanted to discuss in person. The good news was that he would be back tonight and was heading straight to Mia's house. Mia had dropped her daughter off at her parent's home earlier and was now sitting on ready. She was so anxious to speak with Adam.

The doorbell rang, and Mia jumped as if she weren't expecting anyone. She stood, smoothed her clothes, and checked her hair and makeup in the hall mirror before opening the door. Adam stood before Mia with a wide grin on his face. To say that he was pleased to see her or happy to be in her presence would be an understatement.

"Adam, please come in." Mia smiled as she stepped to the side to allow him entrance. Adam stepped through the door and gently closed it, and then greeted Mia with a warm embrace.

"It's good to see you, Mia. How are you doing?"

"I'm pretty good, thank you. Please come on in, make yourself comfortable."

Adam followed Mia through the house and into the family room. They sat comfortably on the couch, probably a little closer than they should have.

"So tell me, what's been going on? What did I miss while I was away?"

"Man-o-man do I have a story to tell you, but before I get into that, can I get you something to eat or drink? I know you came here straight from the airport. You must be starved."

"No thank you, there's no need for you to go to any trouble, I'm fine. Besides, curiosity is killing me," Adam chuckled.

"Well let me not keep you waiting." Mia went on to tell Adam about all that had transpired at the hospital. He seemed just as shocked as Mia was when she watched it all unfold before her eyes.

"Wow, unbelievable. I never would have imagined that this little group I've been investigating was tangled up like this. So this Willow is Wayne's sister, and she is a lesbian. Now although she's gay, she has a child with David. If this isn't some soap opera shit I don't know what is."

"I know, *The Young and The Restless* ain't got nothing on David and this circus he calls his life."

"One thing is for sure; with the information that Willow provided, it shouldn't take any time to get you all that you need for your divorce. To be honest with you, I don't see why David doesn't just sign the papers and give you everything you've asked for. With the mess that he's created, the judge is going to give it to you anyway."

"I don't know Adam. He is still clearly hiding something. The more Willow talked the more hysterical David became. At one point, I thought he would rip her arm out of the socket trying to get her to shut up. He asked her something to the effect of how would Wayne feel if she divulged all of their secrets. We are still missing part of the puzzle."

"Not to worry, I'll find out what it is. I promise. And trust me, it won't take me long."

"I trust you." Mia said softly with an angelic glow lighting her face.

Adam reached over and took Mia's hand. He caressed it softly and was thrilled that Mia did not pull back from him.

"Well, I guess I'd better let you head home. I know you must be tired," Mia spoke softly.

"It is getting late and I certainly don't want to overstay my welcome." Adam stood to his feet and helped Mia to hers. It didn't take but a second for him to pull Mia into his arms. He held her for a brief moment, pulled back a little, and kissed her forehead. "I'll call you tomorrow afternoon, let you know what I find out."

"Okay and thank you for taking the time to come over. I appreciate it."

"Trust me, Mia, it was my pleasure." They walked to the door, embraced once more, and then Adam was gone.

# CHAPTER THIRTY-THREE

Tameka was nearly bouncing off the walls. Ever since the whole hospital scene, her emotions had been completely out of control. Needless to say, Wayne was unable to find a moments peace in his own home. Tameka had badgered him so much about his sister, his friendship with David, and the secrets he was obviously keeping that he was forced to temporarily move out. It was impossible for him to recover from his surgery while sharing space with Tameka.

Tameka had been unable to concentrate on her work and had missed her last two therapy sessions. Every free second she had was spent sitting outside of Wayne's sister's house. She had completely turned into a stalker, and sadly, she didn't really know why. Her relationship with Wayne had changed a long time ago. She was appreciative for his loyalty and dedication to her while she was incarcerated. She cared for his well-being and would always have love for Wayne, but it was not the kind of love that a woman feels for her man. Not the kind of love that evokes thoughts of marriage and children. And it wasn't just the love that was missing but the passion as well. Since her release, Tameka could count the number of times she and Wayne had been intimate on two fingers, and that was fine with them both.

This new found stalker mentality had to derive from Tameka's fear of rejection. The thought of someone not wanting her drove her crazy. Tameka could not fathom that Wayne would want another person more than he wanted her or desire a situation more than he desired the situation that they had. Even though the right kind of love, lust, and desire for Wayne was no longer there, she had to find out what Wayne now wanted more then her.

As Tameka sat in her car watching Willow's front door, her phone rang. Irritated by the noise, Tameka quickly snatched her phone out of her purse. "What is it?" she barked.

"Tameka, this is Connie. Where are you?"

"What do you mean where am I? I'm in my car headed home."

"Tameka, you need to be headed here. You've already missed two sessions. If you do not make it here for today's session, I'll be forced to report you for probation violation. Do you really want to go back to prison for something as minor as this?"

"You can't be serious, Connie?"

"Oh, I'm very serious. So should I expect you within the hour?"

"Connie, I have a lot going on right now. Today just isn't good for me. What if I promise to come in by Friday?"

"If you are not here within the hour, you will be reported and a warrant will be issued for your arrest. Goodbye."

"Fucking bitch!" Tameka screamed as she threw her phone against the car window. She ran her hands through her hair in frustration and reached for the keys to turn the car on. Then just as she lifted her head and looked out across the parking lot, she saw Wayne, Willow and David leaving the condo. Her every impulse and thought was to blow off Connie and follow the Three Musketeers. But a clearer head prevailed and Tameka threw her car into gear and headed to Connie's office.

Tameka huffed her way through the office building and jumped on the elevator. Two minutes later, she walked into

Connie's office and was full of attitude. "Are you happy now? I'm here!"

"Tameka, you need to have a seat and calm down. You also need to understand that you haven't done any favors for me. Your showing up was to save your freedom. It benefits me in no way what-so-ever."

"I can't believe you would have actually turned me in."

"Well believe it. Now, Tameka, tell me what is going on with you. You are clearly on edge and I'm more than a little concerned."

"Save your concern for someone who needs it; I'm fine. I don't understand why you think I'm on edge. Maybe I've just had a hard day. I can't be smiling and sunshine all the damn time."

"Tameka, I don't expect you to be happy and sunny all the time, but something is clearly wrong. You've missed two appointments, your supervisor says that you've been very distracted lately, and your level of agitation is off the charts. So how about we stop beating around the bush and you just come clean with what's going on."

Tameka plopped down in a chair, buried her face in her hands, and began to cry. "Everything is falling apart, Connie. Wayne has moved out of the house, we're not in love anymore. And it's driving me crazy that I don't know who or what has pulled him away from me."

"Why has he moved out Tameka?"

"Connie, it's all so complicated. Wayne has become friends with this guy named David. Turns out that this David guy has a son with Wayne's lesbian sister, whom by the way, I never knew existed. This child has Sickle Cell Anemia and needed a bone marrow transplant. I'll give you one guess as to who his donor was. Now that's all fine and good, but this little circle I just described is keeping some deep secrets between them. Whatever those secrets are, they are pulling Wayne further and further away from me."

"Tameka, you had already acknowledged to me that things were different between you and Wayne before any of this came up. You even went as far as to tell me that you all weren't in love anymore. With this being the case, why do you care so much about the secrets he's keeping or that he moved out? On some level, I would think that you'd be relieved that you didn't have to pretend any longer."

"I'm sorry Connie, things may be different with us, but I still don't like being kept in the dark. Whatever these secrets are, I don't want them exposed, and I end up looking like some kind of fool for being involved with Wayne in the first place."

"As faithful as Wayne was to you during your ordeal, it's hard for me to imagine that he'd turn around and do anything to make you look foolish."

"Okay, fine Connie, he may not make me look like a fool, and even though my love for him has changed, why couldn't…" Tameka's voice trailed off as she fought back tears.

"Why what, Tameka? Finish the question, please."

"Why couldn't he continue to love me like he used to? Why does he feel the need to choose something or someone else over me? Without him, I'll have no one to love me."

There was an uncomfortable silence that settled in the air. For the first time in a long time, Connie was temporarily at a loss for words. Truth be told, Wayne was the only one that cared for Tameka. Her mother had passed, and her brothers were either in prison, out of town or dead. Tameka had no one else to turn to.

Softly, Connie began to speak. "Maybe this is your opportunity to start building new relationships. Your chance to completely let go of your past life and all of those that were a part of it."

"So I should look at this a do-over, right?" Sarcasm dripped from Tameka's tongue.

"I know you're trying to be a wise ass, Tameka, but yes, a do-over."

"Well, Connie, that is one way to look at it. Our session ends in a couple minutes, can we just call it a day right now?"

"One more question, are you going to continue with this investigation of yours?"

"I can't say whether I will or won't at this point, Connie. So much going on in my head; I just need a minute to sort it all out."

"Tameka, just know that if you keep it up, it won't end well. Things like this never end well."

"Goodbye, Connie." Tameka gathered her things and made her exit.

# CHAPTER THIRTY-FOUR

Brook was taking full advantage of her free day while Eric had taken the kids out for a day of fun. He had been jumping in and out of town so much lately that guilt was starting to set in, guilt over not spending enough time with his children or his wife. So Eric told Brook to enjoy her day as long as she was back in time for their date later on that night.

The spa was, indeed, Brooks most relaxing place to spend time when not on vacation. She would start with a deep tissue massage, manicure and pedicure, then on to the facial, and ending of course, with hair and full make-up. Who could ask for more? As soon as she walked in the door, Brook was greeted with hugs and smiles. After exchanging a few pleasantries, she was ushered to a changing room.

Brook was completely relaxed. The day, thus far, had been perfect. They were putting the final touches on her hair and make-up when in walked Tameka. Brook's eyes followed her across the room. "Why the hell can't I escape this witch?" Brook mumbled to herself.

"What did you say, Brook?" the stylist inquired.

"Oh, nothing. Just thinking out loud."

Tameka turned around to sit in her stylist's chair, and that's when she noticed Brook staring holes through her. Tameka tried to ignore her, tried not to meet Brook's gaze. She was determined not to get caught up in any of the mess that had been going on and that included Brook and her desire to protect Mia. Tameka wanted to put forth a real effort to start over just as Connie had suggested.

Brook tried to take her eyes off of Tameka and just pretend that she wasn't there. Her efforts were in vain. She found herself staring in Tameka's direction once again. All she could think about was Tameka's invasion into her children's school. Eric had advised her to let it go, said no harm was done. The kids were never alone with Tameka, and their safety wasn't compromised. He said he didn't want Brook's anger feeding Tameka's fire. It was best to just ignore Tameka and her efforts to get a rise out of them. Brook had agreed but was now finding it impossible to hold her tongue. Her stylist was done and Brook had paid for services rendered. Only one thing left to do.

"Tameka, I'm going to say this one time and one time only, stay the hell away from my children!" Tameka looked up to see Brook barking at her.

"Brook, go away. I don't know what you're talking about, and I don't care to know."

"You know exactly what I'm talking about. The pretend news story you cooked up in order to gain entry to their school. Oh, and let's not forget the message you told my daughter to deliver to me. I just need to be clear; mess with my kids and prison will be the least of your worries. Understand?"

"Go to hell." Tameka growled though clinched teeth.

"Go near my kids again, and it will be you who opens her eyes in hell. I can promise you that." Brook turned on her heels and headed out the door.

Tameka was fuming. She couldn't believe that Brook would have the nerve to confront her in such a public way. It was embarrassing and very much unappreciated. It was this kind of behavior that was going to make it so hard for Tameka to press forward towards a new beginning. Because as hard as Tameka was trying to let go of the past and start over, she knew in her heart that there was no way in hell she would let this little hissy-fit of Brooks go unpunished.

Brook drove through the city replaying the salon incident over and over in her head. Maybe she should have done as Eric instructed and left the situation alone. But, she was a mom, and a real mom stands up for her kids and defends them against any and all potential danger. She only wanted to protect her babies. Now, she worried that her warning was too harsh, too public. Brook shook her head as she remembered that this was crazy ass Tameka she was dealing with. She now hoped that she hadn't made the situation worse.

Eric had been anticipating his wife's return home. He was anxious to get their date night underway. When Brook walked through the door, she was greeted with a warm hug and a beautiful bouquet of roses, her favorite flowers.

"How did you enjoy your day of pampering?" Eric inquired.

"It was fabulous, babe. I feel like a new woman."

"Well, I must say that you look heavenly."

"Oh, you're just saying that because you want hot, steamy sex tonight," Brook mused.

"You darn skippy."

"You're a mess, Mr. Banks. Did you and the kids have fun?"

"We had a ball. Those two are very entertaining. Everything with them was a competition today. All I heard was 'Daddy, didn't I play it better?' 'Daddy, I thought you said I was the best.' It was a mess."

"What did you guys do?"

"We played a little putt-putt golf, spent a short lifetime at Stars and Strikes and finished up at Bruster's. I know we said no sweets, but I just couldn't tell them no with them looking at me with those puppy dog eyes."

"Goodness, you're such a push over."

"Well, this push over has a surprise waiting for you upstairs, so why don't we go get ready and get out of here?"

"Alright, I just want to look in on the kids and then I'm all yours."

Brook stepped into the bedroom and found an amazing cocktail dress, shoes, and handbag waiting for her. She was all smiles. Brook loved it when Eric surprised her. The man had excellent taste, especially in clothes. She had debated whether or not to share today's little incident with Eric, but after all of the trouble he'd gone through to make this a great day for her, she decided against it. Instead, she went out for an amazing evening with her husband and returned home for an even more amazing night of passion.

# CHAPTER THIRTY-FIVE

Adam decided that more aggressive action had to be taken. He had to step his game up in order to get Mia the answers that she was so desperate for. There was so much that Adam wanted to do for Mia but felt that the least he could do for now was provide the information that she was paying him for. She was anxious to get divorced and quite honestly, Adam wanted her to be divorced as well. He felt that that was the only way he had a chance at approaching her in terms of a relationship. There was no mistaking the chemistry between them, but Adam knew that Mia was determined to live a righteous life. He respected her for that and didn't want to do anything to lead her off of that path.

Patiently, Adam waited for David to show up at the condo. Within the hour, David pulled up, parked his car and headed for the front door. Adam grabbed his camera and took off for the back of the building. He found a spot that gave him a bird's eye view into the living area of the condo and another spot gave him a clear shot to the master bedroom. He observed David sifting through a stack of mail. Adam watched as David looked towards the door in response to the doorbell ringing. He took note of the smile that crossed David's face when he discovered it was Wayne on the other side of the door. David greeted his friend with a manly hug and slap on the back. He then stepped to the side to allow Wayne entrance into the house. It wasn't long before the two men were drinking beer and half-heartedly watching a game on television. They seemed much more engrossed in conversation than in the game. This kind of activity went on for what seemed like hours. Eventually, Wayne left and Adam wasn't far behind. Adam's attempt at hard core investigation was a bust. Hopefully tomorrow would bring him better luck.

Mia had put her baby girl to bed, taken a long, hot bath and was now dressed for bed. The only problem, she couldn't sleep. Insomnia had attached itself to her weeks ago and wouldn't let her go. She was finding that her nights were just as long and tiring as her days, but the nights were a lot lonelier. Mia had been depending on her music to keep her company as well as sooth her soul in those midnight hours. Now, that same music just seemed to point out all the miserable aspects of her life or make her long for the touch of a man. There would be no music tonight.

Looking around her bedroom, Mia's eyes fell on the computer and she thought to herself "why not". She padded her way across the room and took a seat in front of the monitor. She preferred using the laptop, but David had taken that one with him. No big surprise that he would take the new computer. He'd tried to take the new stereo equipment and flat screen but, Mia was having none of that. There was no way she would allow him to be rewarded with all of their material possessions after the abandonment of his family. If anything, David should lose everything but the shirt off his back.

Surfing the net wasn't really Mia's thing but it was helping her pass the time. Some of the sites and postings from other people were pretty interesting. She was starting to see why David used to spend so much time on the darn thing. Mia checked out a couple more sites, checked her bank account information and decided that she'd done enough surfing for one night. As she clicked the window closed, a pop up screen appeared. Mia could not believe her eyes. A video of a threesome began to play. Two very buff men with a Barbie Doll type woman were all over each other. Mia hurried and clicked the button to close the window. As soon as she did, another video opened. This time, it was two women and a man going at it and then in walks a second man to join them. Mia scrolled to the bottom of the screen where it was requesting her user name and password. So this is why David lived on that damn computer. Disgusted by what she'd seen, Mia pressed the power button without going through the process of logging off. At this point, she didn't care if she'd messed up files or ruined the thing completely. It was all she could do to keep from throwing it out the window.

The whole internet incident had plagued Mia all morning. She decided that maybe a leisurely lunch with Brook would help her to put it out of her mind. She'd called Brook earlier and of course, her friend did not disappoint. They were scheduled to meet at noon at the Buckhead Diner. Good food and especially good dessert always had a way of perking Mia right up. She checked her watch, 11:30 am, time to head out. She grabbed her purse and advised her assistant that she was leaving. When she arrived at the restaurant, Brook had already arrived and secured them a table.

"Hey, Brook, sorry I'm running late. That lunch time traffic is no joke."

"Who are you fooling, Mia? If there were no traffic at all, you'd still be late. It's in your nature," Brook giggled.

"Don't start with me, girl." Mia warned as she took her seat.

"I see you're a little grumpy today. Do you plan to stay that way for the remainder of the day? Just asking."

"No, didn't mean to sound testy. That's why I asked you to lunch, see if you can help a sistah shake this mood. I hate being all...ugh."

"Ugh? That's an interesting description. Care to explain it?" Brook quizzed as the waiter approached their table.

"Good afternoon, ladies. May I take your drink order?"

"Yes, I'll have a sweet tea with lemon, please," Brook replied.

"I'll have the same."

"Alright and would you care for an appetizer?"

"No, thank you," Mia replied dryly.

"Okay, then I'll be right back with your drinks and take your food order." The waiter turned on his heels and headed towards the back.

"So, what's going on, Mia? I mean, I know what's going on, but there seems to be a little something extra happening here today."

Mia sat in silence for a few moments. She was debating as to whether she wanted to get into the whole computer thing. Her first notion was to avoid the subject and keep lunch drama free. But then she figured that if she couldn't share her true feelings and drama with her best friend, then who could she share them with?

"Last night I decided to do a little web surfing."

"Okay," Brook replied with a question mark in her tone.

"As I was closing the web browser, pop-up windows started coming up one after the other."

"Girl, I hate it when that happens. All those stupid advertisements for everything from vacations to on-line education. They are maddening."

"These were not those types of advertisements, Brook. These were hard core porn pop-up windows. I mean threesomes and foursomes, girl-on-girl and man-on-man and man-on-girl action. It was ridiculous, but most of all, it was hurtful."

"Why was it hurtful, Mia? That spam can get through to anyone's computer."

"The last pop-up box asked for the username and password. That is a serious indicator that the site has been visited by someone that has used my computer. We both know that I rarely use that thing. We also know how much I used to complain about David practically living on it. So it's hurtful to know that my husband chose to spend his time with internet porn as opposed to spending it with me. I don't understand why he would be so caught up in that when he had me, a living, breathing woman right there."

The waiter returned with their beverages and took their food order. The friends sat there for a moment with an uncomfortable silence between them. Brook wanted to say something to sooth her friend, make her feel better, but the right words would not come. Brook decided to speak anyway and hope that she didn't make the situation worse.

"Please understand, Mia, I am in no way trying to defend David. I just want to know if by any chance you know his user name and password? If you do, we can check to see if they work with the site that came up. People usually make the mistake of using the same password for every site. Maybe he did the same. That way we will know for sure if he's guilty of all this porn mess or if there's nothing to it. I don't want to see you feeling hurt over something that may be a none-issue. You have enough to deal with where David is concerned. This may be a worry that we can actually lift off your shoulders."

"I don't know Brook, I could probably figure it out, but what's the point? He has hurt me so much that this would just be a mere drop in the bucket."

"If nothing else, it could give you more ammunition to use against him in the divorce."

Mia thought about what Brook said and it did make perfect sense. She could be worrying for nothing, but if her suspicions were right, this could only help her prove that she is deserving of all that she has asked for in the divorce. "Okay, do you have time to go back to the house with me after lunch?"

"Sure, not a problem," Brook chirped.

"Let me call the office, tell them I won't be back. Thanks, Brook."

Brook smiled lovingly at her friend. They enjoyed their food and much lighter conversation. It wasn't long before Brook was following Mia to her home. It was time for them to get into detective mode. As they approached the house, Mia noticed an unfamiliar vehicle in her driveway and the front door to her house was wide open. Just as she was preparing to call the cops, out walks David carrying the plasma television. Mia throws her car into park and jumps out of the car in a rage. Of course, Brook was hot on Mia's heels, ready to intercede if necessary.

"Just what the hell do you think you're doing?" Mia screamed at the top of her lungs. Did you really think that you were going to prance your ass up in here while I was at work and steal from me?"

"How can I steal what's mine, Mia?"

"You know damn well that we agreed this would stay here with me, so put it back before I call the police, David."

"I wish you would! David exclaimed. My money paid for this and the other stuff that I'm taking out of here. Now get out of my way, Mia."

"The hell I will! Put the TV back, David. I be damned if you're going to walk out on me and my child and then think that you're going to take all of our possessions with you. You must be a bigger fool than I thought."

"Come on guys, y'all don't want to make this situation any worse than it already is." Brook was practically begging.

"Mind your business, Brook," David growled. "Now Mia, I'm not going to tell you again, get out of my way."

"Screw you, David." Mia took out her cell phone and proceeded to call 911. "Yes, I need help. There is an intruder at my home..." Before Mia could finish talking, David snatched her phone and slammed it to the ground. It broke into a million little pieces.

"Why, Mia? Why do you have to make everything so damn difficult?" David's eyes were filled with rage. "That's why you're here by yourself now. You don't know how to just let things alone. You can't let anyone have their way, can't let anybody else be right about nothing, and can't let a man be a man."

"Guys, please back away from this. David, why don't you just leave? Please leave," Brook pleaded.

"Get out of our business, Brook," David demanded as he freed one hand long enough to push Brook away. Without hesitation, Brook turned away with tears in her eyes and dialed 911.

"What the hell is wrong with you, David?" Mia screamed. "Don't you dare put your hands on her like that. Have you lost your mind?"

Instantly, David threw the television to the ground and grabbed Mia around the neck. The more Mia tried to fight him off, the tighter he squeezed. David was determined to choke the very life out of his wife. He gripped her so tight that he lifted Mia right off of her feet. Brook was screaming bloody murder as she tried to make David release Mia from his grip. The weaker Mia seemed to become, the more afraid Brook became. She was hitting David all about his back and head but nothing seemed to deter him from trying to kill Mia. As Brook ran around in circles screaming, she spotted a baseball bat in the garage. Brook ran and grabbed the bat and began to beat the hell out of David. She smacked him in his back so hard that he had no choice but to release Mia. Just as he turned his rage towards Brook, the police came flying down the street with sirens blaring.

# CHAPTER THIRTY-SIX

It was spring break and Kaylie was spending it with her grand-parents. Mia desperately needed time to get her business in order and her mind back on track. After everything that happened with David, she was taking every precaution to make sure that he didn't come near her or their child. Within days of his arrest, she had gone before the court and was granted a temporary order of protection. She knew that it was just a piece of paper, but it made Mia feel a little better. Plus, it provided a paper trail that would be useful during divorce proceedings.

After watching David get carted off to jail, Mia and Brook placed the belongings that David was attempting to take back in their rightful place. That's everything but the television, of course. When all of this started, the plan was to check the computer in hopes of finding out what David had been up to. But, with all the drama, that plan was temporarily put on hold. Today, that hold would be lifted. Adam was on his way over and he would be able to retrieve information from that computer that Mia would never find on her own. The one thing Mia wasn't looking forward to was having to catch Adam up on recent events. She was embarrassed to have to tell anyone about how she was abused by the man that was supposed to love her more than life itself.

The doorbell rang, and Mia, with butterflies in her stomach, trotted to the door to greet Adam. She stepped to the side and motioned with her hand for him to come in. As he crossed the threshold, Mia took note of how good he looked. She caught a whiff of his cologne and got all tingly inside. She had to remind herself that he was there on business and business only. They stepped into the family room and Adam gently grabbed Mia by the hand and pulled her into his arms for a warm embrace. After several seconds, he began to pull away and that's when he noticed the bruises on Mia's neck. Despite the make-up that she had applied, the evidence of her fight with David still came shinning through.

"Mia, what in the world happened to you?"

"Adam, it's a long story."

"I've got nothing but time." Adam motioned for Mia to sit and he took his seat right beside her. "Start talking, young lady."

"Long story short, Brook and I caught David taking things from the house. He and I got into an argument. Brook tried to intervene, and he pushed her. With her out the way, he turned his attention to me and started choking me out. Brook called 911 and ultimately had to beat him with a bat to make him release the grip he had on me. Thankfully, the police arrived pretty quickly and arrested him."

Adam looked enraged. The thought of any man putting his hands on Mia, or any woman for that matter, made him crazy. He had never understood the rage that would drive a man to abuse someone he supposedly cared for.

"Mia, I am so sorry. I'm sorry that I wasn't here to protect you from him. I'm sorry that I haven't given you more information on David's actions. I don't know what else to say except I'm sorry."

"Adam, you have nothing to apologize for. None of this is any of your fault. No one had any reason to think that David would ever do anything like this. Until now, abuse has not been a part of our history. I never imagined that David would put his hands on me in that manner."

"Still, I should have been the one to protect you."

"Adam, I don't think that that is part of your job description," Mia chuckled.

"Doesn't have to be part of the job. Protecting you is what my heart tells me to do."

The look on Mia's face told Adam that she may not have been ready to hear such a strong comment. But it was getting harder and harder for him to hide the way he felt about her.

"I apologize. I shouldn't have said that. I didn't mean to make you uncomfortable."

"I'm not uncomfortable at all," Mia mumbled with a sly grin.

Adam was pleasantly surprised by Mia's response but didn't know if he should continue this flirting game. He in no way wanted to disrespect Mia, so he turned the conversation back to David.

"Do you know if he's still locked up?"

"I heard that he's been released. No doubt his baby's mama bailed him out."

"Hmm, I'm not so sure about that. By morning, I'll have all the details regarding who posted bail, the terms of the bail, and his future court dates."

"Thanks, I'll be waiting to hear the details." Mia shifted in her seat, a little unsure of how her next question would be received. "Adam, I know that we are supposed to be discussing David and all, but would you mind if we shifted gears a bit? I'm worn out with reliving the events of the past couple of days."

"Of course I don't mind, but do you still want me to gather the information from the computer?"

"How about I let you take it with you when you leave, and once you've accessed the information, you can share your findings with me?"

"Of course, it's not a problem." With much hesitation, Adam stood to his feet. "Well, I won't keep you."

"Oh no, I didn't want you to leave. I just don't want to talk about David anymore." Mia stated as she jumped to her feet. "And I don't know about you, Adam, but I'm starving. Do you mind if we go grab a bite to eat?"

"Not at all," Adam replied with a little too much excitement in his voice. "What are you in the mood for?"

"Something that we can get to go. I really want to come back here, eat, and relax."

"Sounds like a plan to me."

The pair headed out the door with much more than dinner on their minds. Adam couldn't help thinking how attracted he was to Mia. He wanted to be her protector, her supporter, her friend, and yes, her lover. Mia couldn't deny her increasing attraction to Adam. He was a physically and mentally strong man. Adam represented what Mia felt she was missing in her life. A man to listen to her, not try and fix her but, just listen. She wanted a man to understand her and accept her as she was. Mia wanted a man that would love her inside and out and make her feel like the only woman that mattered to him. But the fact of the matter remained that Mia was still married. So despite what she wanted, she was stuck with the task of honoring her vows until the court system set her free.

Adam was back the next evening with Mia's computer in hand. He was pleased to see Brook at the house visiting with Mia. He had nothing but more bad news and knew that Mia would need to be comforted by someone that she knew was on her side.

"Hello, ladies. How are you all doing this evening?"

"I'm just fine," Brook replied with a broad smile.

"And you, Mia?" Adam was trying to gauge Mia's state of mind.

"I'm wonderful, Adam. How are you today?"

"I'm good."

Everything about Adam's tone and demeanor told Mia that something was definitely wrong. He had information that he didn't want to have to share with her, something that could potentially hurt her heart. It was clearly written all over his face.

"Mia, where can I set this computer up?"

"Let's take it to the kitchen. How bad is it, Adam?"

Adam silently moved through the house and into the kitchen. He went about the business of setting up the computer without once looking up at Mia, never making eye contact. This evasive behavior put Mia on pins and needles. She didn't know what to expect, but she knew that whatever it was it would be the final nail in the coffin that would bury her marriage for good. Sensing the intensity of the situation, Brook asked if she should leave and give them a chance to sort through whatever the information was. Without giving Mia a chance to reply, Adam mumbled, "I think you should stay. The information is quite sensitive and embarrassing, but Mia will need your support."

"You heard the man. Sit on down and let's see what's going on." Mia's voice was trembling with fear and nerves.

With everyone sitting and anxiously waiting, Adam turned the computer on and started opening files. "Ladies, these are video files, and I ask that you forgive me for viewing the content and for having to share it with you." The first file opened and Adam clicked play. It was a sex video of David and his baby's mother, Willow. They were going at it like nobody's business. Mia sat there watching the video and thinking about how long it had been since her husband had even approached her for sex, let alone show her the passion that he was displaying on the video. Just as Mia was about to announce that she had seen enough, another woman appeared on the screen. It was Pam, the woman that Willow had introduced as her girlfriend. It was now a full on threesome.

Mia shook her head in disgust, "Wow, he got to fulfill the fantasy that every man seems to have."

"Not every man," Adam assured.

"Are you okay, Mia?" Brook quizzed.

"Yes, I'm…I'm okay. Is that it, can we turn this off now?"

Adam spoke hesitantly "I'm afraid not. There is more and I think that you need to know about it all." With that said, Adam opened a second file and clicked play. There was David with his back to the camera. He was obviously kissing someone. As their bodies turned in unison, it was clear to see that the passionate kiss he was sharing was with a man. But not just any man; it was Wayne. They kissed, touched, and ultimately began to have sex. Mia jumped from the table, ran to the bathroom, and emptied her stomach into the commode.

# CHAPTER THIRTY-SEVEN

Tameka had all but given up on her attempts to catch Wayne in some incriminating situation. She had been staking out that condo for weeks and kept coming up empty handed. She knew he was hiding something but decided to move on, trusting that his secrets would soon be revealed. However, she had not given up on her quest to seek revenge on Brook. Quite honestly, she wasn't sure she wanted revenge. What Tameka desired most was respect. Since her release, she had followed the rules, reignited her career and kept to herself. But, Brook still wouldn't leave her alone. She took advantage of every possible opportunity that presented itself to humiliate Tameka. Brook seemed to get a kick out of publicly berating her. But that would have to stop.

It was a beautiful day, and Tameka was looking forward to all of the tasks that lay before her. She was rushing to get out the door. A news piece that she had produced alone was airing today. It was an investigation into the corruption that was taking place in one of the major counties. Tameka also knew that they would announce the new executive producer of a political satire show that was going to debut in the fall. If her news piece today was well-received, then she fully expected to land the executive producer gig.

Tameka rushed into the station with the excitement of a kid going to the circus. She met with the news anchor that would do the introduction for her piece. Tameka wanted to make sure that the woman was familiar and comfortable with the subject matter. Not that it would make a bit of difference, but the chat just seemed to make Tameka feel better and that was enough for the anchor to sit and listen to Tameka with a smile on her face. She knew how much the story meant to Tameka. As the twelve o'clock hour approached, Tameka went and joined her manager in one of the offices where they would view the story as it aired. Tameka's confidence was unshakable. She worked on the piece, checking and double checking all the facts and making sure that every single detail was on point.

"I have to give it to you, Tameka, that was excellent work. Since coming on board here, you have really stepped up to the plate and proved yourself worthy. I expect that big things will continue to happen for you."

"Thank you, Mrs. Gillman. I'm glad I was able to produce a strong piece for the station, and I will continue to give you all my very best."

"I have no doubt about that, Tameka. Well, I know you have an appointment, so go ahead and take off, and I'll see you a little later on."

"Alright, I won't be gone too long," Tameka almost sang. She was beyond pleased with the way things were going, and though she wasn't looking forward to her next task, she knew it was something that had to be done.

Sitting across the street from the school playground, Tameka would have a clear view of the children as they came out for recess. She had sat outside the school enough times to know that she only had about a five minute wait before the kids would began to spill out of the door. Tameka had a brief thought that maybe she shouldn't be there. Maybe Brook wasn't worth her trouble. "Get your head in the game, Tameka. This is exactly where you need to be," she spoke to herself in a calm and soothing voice. She was fully prepared to follow through with her plan. Tameka looked in the backseat of her car to make sure she had everything. There on the seat lay a new princess doll, a child's sweater, and a paper bag filled with snacks. All she needed now was the little girl.

The side doors to the school flew open and out ran the kids from several classrooms. Tameka surveyed the area. There was only one slim guy near the corner, no one else was around. She stood outside of her car and looked for Brook's daughter. There she was, that pretty little girl playing near the edge of the property with her friend. The other little girl jumped up and ran off, and Tameka knew that her opportunity was at hand. She began to slowly walk across the street when she noticed the slim guy from the corner moving hastily towards the child that she herself was after. What in the hell was he doing? What was happening? The questions raced through Tameka's mind. The man slowed his pace and stalked Brook's daughter as if he were a lion and she was an innocent gazelle. Then suddenly, he ran onto the school property, snatched his prey, and began to run with the screaming child.

All hell broke loose. The teachers started screaming for help while trying to usher the other kids back into the building. One heavy set woman began to give chase but it was clear that she wouldn't be able to catch the pervert as he made his escape with the child. As he approached the woods, it hit Tameka that if he disappeared into the brush area, that that child would never be seen alive again. Tameka reached back into her car, grabbed her stun gun, and took off. Thankfully, the little girls kicking and hitting slowed the abductor down giving Tameka a chance to catch up. When she was within arm's length, Tameka grabbed the man's shirt, trying to pull him to the ground. Still holding to the girl, he pushed Tameka's hand away. She ran faster, and instead of grabbing his shirt, she reached out and pressed the stun gun into his back. The shock caused him to fall to the ground with the girl. Tameka pulled the girl away from him, and then shocked him again and again to ensure that he wouldn't immediately get up.

Within minutes, the police had converged on the scene. Tameka walked back towards the school campus holding the little girl safely in her arms while the cops took the abductor into custody. School officials tried to take the girl, but she held on to Tameka's neck and refused to let her go. Even Tameka couldn't pry the sobbing child's hands from around neck. It wasn't until a panic stricken Brook pulled up and ran over to the scene that the girl let go.

"Mommy, Mommy!" Kristen screamed.

"I'm right here, baby, Mommy's right here." Brook cried as she snatched her child away from Tameka. Thankfully, looks couldn't kill because if they could, Tameka would've been dead on the spot. "What did you do to my baby?" Brook spat at Tameka. "What did you do? If you hurt one hair on her head, I will kill you. Do you hear me, I will kill you!"

"Mrs. Banks, that's enough," the principal scolded as she stepped between Brook and Tameka. "Instead of accusing this woman, you should be thanking her. She just saved your child's life."

Confusion crept across Brook's face. She couldn't believe what she was hearing. Then she saw the cops lift someone to their feet and usher him to a waiting cop car. "I...I don't understand?" Brook stammered as she tried to console her daughter.

"That man in handcuffs grabbed your daughter and took off running. Ms. Williams here gave chase and was able to stun the perpetrator long enough to get the little one back and for the police to take him into custody." The principal then turned her attention to Tameka. "Ms. Williams, while I do not appreciate your lying to me a few weeks ago about who you were, I am eternally grateful for your heroism. Thank you." The woman gave Tameka a warm embrace and then walked off to speak with the police.

Brook looked at Tameka with confusion still in her eyes.

Before she could collect her thoughts or begin to speak, ambulance workers were in their faces asking if either Tameka or the child were injured. Tameka assured them that she was fine. They did insist on taking Brook's daughter to the hospital as a precaution. Mother and daughter were ushered off to a waiting ambulance as the media converged on the scene. For the second time in her life, Tameka was going to be the top news story of the day. From the back of the ambulance, Brook looked on, still in a state of disbelief.

# CHAPTER THIRTY-EIGHT

Tameka decided to go in late the next morning. Thankfully her manager was fine with it given the circumstances of the previous day. The turn of events had left Tameka a little shaken, and she thought it best to talk things over with Connie. She needed a little reassurance to help her get her footing back. Driving through town in complete silence was not her thing, so Tameka reached and turned on the radio. She was shocked to hear that she was the topic of conversation for the day. The host and his sidekicks were discussing her past transgressions and if her actions of yesterday, in addition to her prison time, proved that she was now an honorable and respectable woman.

The reviews were mixed. One of the personalities felt that she was a murderer and that one act of bravery wouldn't change who or what she truly was. The other two felt that she had paid her debt to society and that yesterday's incident proved that she was now a decent, contributing member of society. Then the listeners started calling in with their opinions. It was more than Tameka could take, and she decided to drive in silence after all. It wasn't long before she was pulling into the parking garage.

"Hi Connie, thanks for seeing me on such short notice."

"You're welcome. I'm glad you called. It saved me a trip."

"What do you mean?" Tameka asked as she made herself comfortable.

"Well, I was planning to drop by your job today. After yesterday, I knew that we would need to talk. So tell me, how are you feeling?"

"You have to keep everything I say confidential. You remember that, right?"

"Of course I do, Tameka. But thanks for the reminder," Connie quipped.

"The police wanted to know what I was doing at the school in the first place. I told them that I was there to follow up on a previous visit I'd made. Told them I was working on a story about public versus private schools."

"Okay, I'm sure everyone was glad you were there regardless of the reason."

"But that was a lie, Connie. I was there to kidnap that girl myself." Tameka burst into sobs. "I was going to take her and ride her around for a while and then drop her off near her neighborhood. I wasn't going to hurt her. I just wanted to scare Brook. Show her that I'm not to be disrespected or screwed with."

"Tameka, what were you thinking? Do you know the kind of trouble you would have been in? Look how much progress you have made. You would have thrown it all away and been shipped back off to prison. How in the world do you think that something so crazy would have earned you anyone's respect?"

"Connie, please! I realize all of that now. I know that it was a stupid idea. But don't you see the bigger picture here?"

"Please, Tameka, show me the bigger picture."

"The bigger picture is that God stepped in and gave me an opportunity to turn my bad into good. I was given a chance to be a little girl's hero. I could have let that man take her and save me the trouble. Brook would have suffered far more by his actions than she would have by mine. But when I saw him snatch her, I knew that he would kill her, and that was unacceptable to me. It was unacceptable." Tameka wiped her eyes, but the tears kept flowing.

"So what does that tell you about yourself, Tameka?"

"I'm not the evil person that everyone made me out to be. I'm not the damaged woman that I thought I was."

"No, Tameka, you aren't damaged or evil. You have made some very poor choices in life, but you have the power to change the path that you've been on. You are capable of living a good, respectable life. You are far more than you've ever given yourself credit for."

"Most of all, Connie, I've finally given my mother a reason to be proud. Too bad she isn't here to see the good I've done."

"I'm sure that her spirit is smiling on you as we speak."

The drive into work was much better than the ride to Connie's office. Tameka felt as if the world had been lifted from her shoulders. She did not realize how heavy her anger and resentment towards Brook was. It had been weighing her down for so long that she'd forgotten what it felt like not to carry that load. As dangerous as the previous day's events were, it was something that had to happen in order to set Tameka free. That one moment of truth had done more for her than eight years of prison ever could. Tameka knew that she was worthy, worthy of love and respect. She no longer had to fight, plot, and scheme to be viewed in a positive light. Tameka was already standing in the light and whoever didn't want to acknowledge that, well that was their loss, and Tameka refused to be fazed by their negativity ever again.

Walking into work was a little nerve racking. Butterflies were in her stomach only because she didn't know what to expect. Was her job in jeopardy because she'd lied about where she was going? Tameka just didn't know what was awaiting her. Needless to say, she was floored by the flowers and balloons, the cheers and the clapping. Her heart soared.

Brook spent the day cuddling and loving on her children. She had spent the night crying in the arms of her husband. Eric had flown back home yesterday evening as soon as he'd heard the news. He was so angry, mostly with himself, for not being there to protect his family. His daughter could have been killed, and there he was, off talking business on a damn golf course. How could he have been so negligent? Brook, on the other hand, was conflicted. She was furious with Tameka for being at her children's school because she knew in her heart that Tameka was plotting something evil. At the same time, she was grateful for Tameka. She was grateful that Tameka was in the right place at the right time and that she'd made the right decision.

Brook put the kids down for a nap and went into the kitchen to fix some herbal tea. Eric entered the kitchen behind her and took a seat at the bar. A couple of minutes passed before he began to speak. "So, how do you think we should handle things as they pertain to Tameka?"

"What do you mean? There is nothing to handle with her."

"Brook, I don't like or trust her either. I have never and will not in the future want her to be a part of our lives. But, the fact remains that she did save our child's life. The story is all over the media and isn't going to go away anytime soon. If we don't issue some type of thank you to her, we will be the ones that look bad. They will drag us through the mud for our ungratefulness."

"I'm sorry, Eric, but I'm having a hard time trying to convince myself that she is worthy of our thanks and appreciation. I can't shake the feeling that she was up to no good when the chance to do something good just happened to fall in her lap. We both know that she wouldn't spit on me if I were on fire, so why would she put herself in harm's way like that to save my child? It makes no sense to me."

"I understand, Baby. I really understand how you feel. But the fact remains that she did protect, rescue, save our little girl. As much as I hate everything she stands for, I am and will always be eternally grateful. And that is what we need to express in a public statement. If we don't, that media circus that's camped out in front of the house will never leave."

"Fine, let them know that we will address them in a half hour. That will give me enough time to make myself look presentable and the kids will still be asleep."

"Alright."

Eric called to the security gate and asked the officer on duty to advise the media that they were ready to speak. Within minutes, their front lawn was covered with news reporters from local stations as well as the national morning shows. It was insane. Shortly before they were prepared to speak, they heard the doorbell ring. The sound angered Brook. She thought it was unbelievably rude of the media to try and rush them out. She was prepared to hurt someone's feelings, but after looking through the glass door, she relaxed and carefully opened it enough to let Mia squeeze in.

"Girl, I'm so glad to see you," Brook almost sang.

"I would've been here sooner but do you know what a mad house it has been here? Trying to push passed the sea of television reporters was absolutely crazy."

"Yes, I know. We are actually getting ready to address them all."

"Okay, do you know what you're going to say?"

"Honestly, I'm going to let Eric take the lead. He's basically going to say how grateful we are to Tameka for her heroic act."

"Brook, if you could hear the hatred that drips from your tongue when you speak of Tameka, you'd go running off to the River Jordan for a dip in the waters of forgiveness."

"What the hell do you mean by that? She's the one who needs the forgiveness. She's the evil one here, remember?"

"Yes, Brook, I remember. I know what she did to you. I witnessed the pain you suffered first hand. But I also know that you have got to let go of this anger and hatred that you have for her."

"Give me one good reason why. Why should I not hold her

accountable for what she took from me, Mia? She took my baby."

"And yesterday she gave you your other baby back."

"So is that supposed to erase everything she did before? I don't think so. Tameka Williams is still an evil, sneaky, underhanded snake and I will never make the mistake of forgetting that."

"Brook, the word forget has never once crossed my lips. I said that you have to let it go. You have to forgive. This is something that you will have to do for you. By carrying this around, you're only condemning yourself. Now I don't know about you, but I don't need any help from anybody getting into hell. I have enough to account for without holding on to hatred because of something somebody did to me."

"Fine, Mia, you just remember all this crap you're talking when your personal life and all that David has done to you is put on public display. I want to see this forgiving attitude when you're sitting there in divorce court."

"Wow, I think it's time for me to go. Good luck with everything." Mia turned and headed out of the house. Brook called after her but it was in vain. Mia kept right on stepping.

Several minutes later, Brook stood by her husband's side as he addressed the media. She smiled politely, trying to look genuine as Eric expressed their appreciation for all that Tameka had done. When Eric spoke of Tameka's bravery and the unselfishness of her acts, it was all Brook could do to keep from throwing up. The words that she really wanted to speak about Tameka were literally burning her throat. Brook was so relieved when Eric wrapped up his message, and they returned to the interior of their home.

"See, babe, we have that behind us now. They can just replay that little press conference over and over again. We won't be accepting any invitations to do talk shows or anything of the sort," Eric reassured.

"I'm glad it's all over. Our kids are safe and nothing more needs to be said about Tameka."

"True. But Brook, there is more that needs to be said."

"What do you mean, Eric?"

"I heard yours and Mia's conversation, and you were dead wrong. I can't believe some of the things you said to her. I'm the first to admit that Tameka has done some horrible things to you, to us for that matter, but I never thought you would allow her behavior to change who you are. You're becoming a cold woman, Brook, and you're turning on the friend that has always been in your corner. I love you, baby but you need to check yourself." Eric then turned and walked out of the room, leaving Brook to ponder his words.

# CHAPTER THIRTY-NINE

It was the morning of Mia and David's final court hearing. Mia fully expected for the divorce to be granted and for her to receive everything that she'd asked for. Adam would be in the courtroom to lend his moral support. As Mia's investigator, he had been there to give his testimony but stayed away the rest of the time. He didn't want anyone to become suspicious of his feelings for the plaintiff. Mia always assumed that Brook would be there in support of her as well, but with things going the way that they had recently, she had dropped all expectations of Brook showing up.

Proceedings were just about to begin when Brook eased through the door. She quietly took a seat near the back, going unnoticed by everyone in the room. The bailiff called the court to order, the judge took his seat, and Mia braced herself for what he was about to say.

"This won't take long, folks. Over the last few days, I've listened to testimony, viewed pictures, and heard every request made by each side in these proceedings. Honestly, after the first thirty minutes of the first day, I could have rendered my decision. But I listened to everything just in case something was said to change my mind. It wasn't. Everything that I've heard only cemented my first thoughts about this case. Mrs. Purcell, I commend you for being the unbreakable woman and tremendous mother that you clearly are. I wish you only happiness and peace for your future. Mr. Purcell, there are no kind words that can be spoken about you. You are a sad excuse for a man, husband, and father. With that being said, I grant Mrs. Purcell her divorce. She will have sole custody of the child. Mr. Purcell will be allowed supervised visitation. Upon completion of a court approved anger management class and his probation for the attack on his wife, a request can be filed for more liberal visitation. Mrs. Purcell will retain the family home, all of its contents, and her vehicle. Mr. Purcell is ordered to pay child support in the amount of $1,450.00 monthly and is further ordered to pay Mrs. Purcell $36,000.00 which is approximately half of his 401k investment fund. All other jointly held stocks and bonds are to be divided equally. Court is adjourned." With a hit of the judge's gavel, it was over and Mia was free to make a new life for herself.

Mia almost jumped out of her seat, excited with the judgment and about her future. David on the other hand was still sitting at the table with his head in his hands. Mia thanked her lawyer, turned and leaped into Adam's arms. He embraced her with more warmth and happiness than Mia had felt in a long time. When Adam finally released her, Mia looked around and saw Brook standing in the courtroom with a smile as big as Texas plastered across her face. The friends walked to one another and hugged as if no harsh words had ever been passed.

"Mia, I'm so happy for you. You deserve everything you were awarded and more. Now you get to start over and live the life you've longed for."

"Thank you, Brook. Thank you for coming."

"You know that I love you, right?

"Yes, I know."

"And I am so sorry for the way I talked to you and for the

things I said. I allowed my anger and hatred for Tameka to get the better of me. I promise it will never happen again."

"Brook, it's okay, apology accepted. Now let's forget about all that mess and move on," Mia sang. Then she, Brook and Adam started on their way out of the court room. Just as they were getting ready to cross the threshold, David called out to Mia.

"I'm sorry, Mia, I'm sorry for everything. I never meant to hurt you and you know that I never wanted to hurt our little girl. My children are my life and I'm begging you, please let me explain to Kaylie why I won't be around like I used to? Please?"

"No, I can't allow that. I explained all of that to Kaylie months ago when you first stopped spending time with her. She already understands that you won't be around and has already begun to adjust. I won't allow you to screw with her anymore." Mia and her small entourage of supports turned and walked away.

# CHAPTER FORTY

The alarm blared and Tameka slowly turned over in bed to turn it off. She had every intention of getting up bright and early and driving to the east side of town. She'd promised her co-workers that she would meet them at Stone Mountain for an early morning climb. That wasn't going to happen. Tameka had been pushing herself harder than ever on the job, and she was too tired to climb anyone's mountain today. She turned over and quickly fell back asleep.

Once again, a blaring noise snatched Tameka from dreamland. As she sat up in bed, she realized that this noise was different, this time it was the security alarm. Tameka jumped out of bed and went for her stun gun. Then she heard a couple of beeps, and the deafening noise stopped. A couple of seconds later, Wayne stepped into the bedroom.

"Tameka, would you please put that thing away?"

"What the hell are you doing here, Wayne?"

"If I'm not mistaken, this is still my house. I mean, I know I haven't been around a lot but still."

"If that's not the understatement of the year, I don't know what is. So are you back here to stay or just to pick up a few more of your things?"

"I came to talk to you, if that's okay?"

"What do we need to talk about, Wayne? I've kind of figured it all out. You and your best friend David decided that the women in your lives weren't good enough for you anymore, and you've chosen new ones. Well if you think some new chick is going to make you happier than I do, go for it. Don't let me stand in your way."

"Tameka, we really need to talk. I'd like to explain things before you hear about it all elsewhere. How about I put on a pot of coffee while you get yourself together?"

"Fine, I don't see the point of all this, but fine."

Tameka went to the restroom to freshen up while Wayne made his way into the kitchen. He had practiced how he would break the news to Tameka. He'd rehearsed the words over and over again. But now that the time was here, the words he'd practiced were leaving him fast. He was so nervous that his hands were trembling. Wayne felt that if he could come clean with Tameka, then doing so with the other people in his life would be a snap.

"So start talking," Tameka demanded as she plopped down at the table.

Wayne served the coffee and took a seat on the other side of the table. With a slight tremble in his voice, Wayne began to slowly unveil his truth. "Tameka, there is no other woman. You have been the only woman in my life for years now. But, there are things that I've been trying to deal with and for the first time in a long time, I have clarity about who I am."

"And who are you, Wayne?"

"I am a man that has accepted myself for what I am."

"Okay, stop playing games. What are you, besides annoying?"

"I'm gay."

"Excuse me?"

"I'm gay, Tameka."

Tameka sat there like a stone statue. Her head tilted to the side, she stared at Wayne the way one might stare at a Martian. Finally, she snapped out of her trance and her words returned to her. "Wayne, is it really necessary for you to lie about your sexuality? If you want to formally call this thing we have or had off, at least be man enough to stand up and say that's what you want. Only a punk ass excuse of a man would go to this extent just to end a relationship."

"It's not an excuse, Tameka. This is something that I've been struggling with for years. I always thought that the right woman would be able to kill my desires for men. Then I met you. You were beautiful, smart, successful, and I even enjoyed our sex life, something I'd never enjoyed with any other woman."

"Well if I fixed you, what makes you think you're gay now?"

"Like I said, it's something I've always struggled with. But when we were together, I was able to push those feelings to the back of my mind. I was able to suppress those feelings. Then you went away, and I was left alone."

"So my going to prison made you gay. Do you know how stupid this shit sounds?" Tameka was losing her patients, and her voice was starting to tremble with anger.

"Please stay calm. I really don't want this to get ugly. I'm just trying to be honest with you, and trust me, it's a lot harder than you know."

"Oh, poor Wayne. He's decided to step out of the closet and leave me. Please tell me Wayne, have you acted on these gay tendencies?"

"Yes," Wayne confessed as he dropped his head and began to silently weep.

"Are you freaking kidding me? Your ass has screwed another man and now you're crying about it. What kind of bitch ass mess is this? Are you seriously telling me that I've been screwing a man who's also been screwing a man? I should kill you right now! I swear. I should slit your throat and watch your punk ass bleed to death. I hate you! How could you do this to me?"

Wayne was all out sobbing now and pleading with Tameka

for mercy. "Baby, I swear I never meant for any of this to happen. I never meant to hurt you."

"Did you really just have the nerve to call me *baby*?"

Defeated, Wayne dropped back down in his seat. "I'm sorry. I don't know what else to say except I'm sorry."

"I got to get out of here. I can hardly breathe. I need air." Tameka grabbed her keys and jetted out of the door. She drove around with no destination, and it wasn't until she flew past a cop that she realized she didn't have her license. That realization sent her back in the direction of the home that she shared with Wayne. She knew that he was still there, still waiting to finish their conversation. But she didn't know how much more she could handle without snapping. The only thing holding her back from wreaking havoc on Wayne was all that she stood to lose if she did. She refused to give up her freedom for this confused jackass. Tameka pulled into the driveway and sat for a bit. She took a few deep breaths and returned to the house with only two questions for Wayne. Once she was satisfied with his answers, she would be done with him and all that he represented.

"I didn't think that you'd come back so soon," Wayne droned.

"I just have two questions for you, Wayne and then I'm done with all of this and with you. Did you have unprotected sex with you male partners?"

"Absolutely not. I would never be that irresponsible or do anything that would put our health at risk. And there has only been one person," Wayne explained.

"That's question number two. Do I know this lover of yours? Who is he?"

Wayne dropped his head and mumbled, "David."

"David who?" Tameka demanded.

"David Purcell, Mia's husband."

Tameka's mouth dropped open, but no words would come out. She was in a semi-state of shock. She knew that David and Wayne shared a connection, but never really believed that this was it. "But David isn't gay. He has another girlfriend, your sister, remember? They just had a child together. He isn't gay."

"Remember, my sister is a lesbian. She and her girlfriend wanted a baby and David was kind enough to give them the opportunity to be parents. Plus, he wanted another shot at having a son. Mia refused to get pregnant again for fear that the child would have Sickle Cell Anemia. She couldn't bear to lose another baby to that horrific disease. So this was the perfect solution for both David and my sister. And for the record, David does not consider himself gay."

"Well what the hell does he think he is?" Tameka quizzed with a look of confusion painted across her face.

"He still considers himself straight. In his eyes, being with another man is a type of fetish. It's not something he wants all the time, just every now and then. Sadly, he's not ready to accept who or what he truly is." Wayne's voice cracked with that last sentence. He seemed hurt by the knowledge that David wouldn't accept ownership of his obvious homosexuality.

"You are so pathetic and I'm sorry, but I can't seem to muster up any sympathy for you. I'll be out of your house within the next couple of weeks."

"No need to rush, you can stay as long as you need to."

Monday morning found Tameka still in a haze. She was working hard, and getting things done, but she wasn't her usual chipper self and everyone seemed to notice.

"Tameka, could I see you in my office for a moment?" Mrs. Gillman requested.

"Of course," Tameka placed an armful of papers on her desk and stepped across the hall to her manager's office.

"Is everything okay, Tameka? You seem really out of it." Mrs. Gillman quizzed.

"Yes, I'm okay, have some things on my mind, but I can

assure you that I won't let it affect my work."

"That is not a concern of mine. Your work is exceptional, and it hasn't gone unnoticed. A Houston station seems to think that you could have mass appeal and that your recent heroic activity could only add to your popularity. They want to do a profile piece on you to introduce you to the Houston community, and then move you into the lead anchor position."

"Oh my goodness, are you serious?" Tameka was in a complete state of shock.

"Very serious. They have experienced a slip in their ratings and seem to think that you could help win their audience back."

Tameka plopped down in the chair, trying to absorb everything that Mrs. Gillman had said. "Houston, huh?"

"How do you feel about relocating?" Mrs. Gillman inquired.

"Funny you should ask. I have to move anyway; it may as well be out of state. My only concern is my probation. I don't know how likely the state is to allow me to leave."

"Well, I took the liberty of speaking with your parole officer, and he seems to believe that the state would be willing to transfer your probation obligation to the state of Texas. Especially if Connie is willing to speak on your behalf."

"I am so blown away right now. I don't even know what to say."

Mrs. Gillman chuckled, "Well you better figure out what to say pretty quickly because they want to send one of their news personalities here this week to do the profile piece."

Tameka giggled her way back to her desk. The things that Connie said were really true. Tameka was being given an opportunity to start over. She called Connie as soon as she sat down. Tameka valued Connie's opinion and wanted to know what she thought of the offer that she'd been presented with. Connie suggested that Tameka make a list of all the reasons she had to stay in Atlanta and all the reasons that she had to leave. Tameka did just that, and then she examined the lists and made her decision.

# CHAPTER FORTY-ONE

It had been three weeks since Mia was granted her freedom. She'd happily packed up everything that belonged to David and was thrilled when he'd picked all that crap up. A makeover was what she'd decided to give the house. A new look for a new beginning. Naturally, Kaylie still had some adjusting to do, but that little girl was tickled pink when Mia told her that she'd get to redecorate her room. She'd picked pink and purple as her room colors and was getting a brand new, queen sized bed. Yes, she was happy with that, and Mia would love her through this transition period.

Mia was also excited about her date tonight. Of course it was with Adam. Those feelings that they had begun to have for one another prior to her divorce had not gone away. If anything, they'd intensified. But Mia had made it perfectly clear that she wasn't looking for anything serious. She was still dealing with the way things ended with David. The love they'd shared had died a while ago, but she was still hurt that he'd turned to someone else for companionship. And to find out that the other person was a man was almost more than Mia could bear. Once it sank in that her husband had been with another man, Mia made an immediate appointment with her gynecologist. Thank God she was disease-free. It was the reality of all that drama that had Mia wanting to move slowly and cautiously with Adam.

"Where are my keys?" Mia questioned herself as she scurried around the house looking for the elusive keys. She had an early brunch and shopping date with Brook and didn't want to be late. Finally, she found the keys in her jacket pocket. She hated when she did that and tried to be diligent about putting her keys in her purse. Obviously, she didn't try hard enough. Mia bolted out the door and jumped in the car. She paused long enough to load a couple of good CD's into the CD changer. Good riding music was a must, even if she was only riding across town. Maxwell began to sing about his woman's *Pretty Wings,* and Mia started singing along as she took off down the street.

"You're late," Brook scorned as she stood in the doorway. "And you're without Kaylie."

"Are you going to let me in or just stand there fussing like you're my momma?"

Brook stepped aside to allow Mia entrance into her home. Mia pranced in and went straight to the kitchen. "May I please have some water?"

"Since when did you start asking? You see that big contraption over there? It's called a refrigerator; help yourself."

"You sure have a lot of mouth going on today. Am I going to have to listen to you be a wise apple all day?"

"Oh lighten up! Finish your water and let's go."

"Do you mind if I say hi to the family first?"

"Girl, Eric is gone for the day, and the kids are sleep. Now let's go."

"I get the feeling that this is going to be a long day." Mia mumbled as she made her way out of the front door.

Driving through town, listening to music, and sharing silly conversation was all it took to make a picture perfect afternoon for the friends. Brunch at the Ritz was fabulous, as usual. Mia and Brook ate until they thought they would burst. The shopping would have to wait for a bit. Neither felt that they could move a muscle until their stomachs settled. The way they had eaten was sinful, but it sure was good. Finally, they gathered themselves and headed for Phipps Plaza. It was officially time to spend some money.

"Isn't this gorgeous?" Mia quizzed.

"Wow! That's pretty hot. Any special reason you're looking at all this lingerie?"

"No," Mia protested. "We all need underwear, may as well make it pretty. Besides, who wants to wear granny panties? Certainly not me."

"Are you sure that this little trip through the lingerie department has nothing to do with Adam?" Brook continued to push at Mia's buttons.

"Brook, you have been throwing hints all day about me and Adam being intimate. Now I'll be the first to admit that we are crazy attracted to one another, but I don't think we're ready for the sex stuff yet."

"Do you know if Adam feels the same way about it that you do?"

"In all honesty, it doesn't matter how he feels about it. My body, my decision. I say we wait and see where this little relationship leads us." Mia continued to browse through the negligees. She picked up one after the other. She favored the ones with lace. After choosing a few sexy pieces, she moved on to the panties and bras. Brook patiently watched as Mia very carefully made her selections. Brook could not help but smile as she watched Mia go about her shopping.

"Brook, why are you starring and grinning at me like that?"

"Oh, I'm sorry. I didn't realize I was starring. But you know, I must admit that I'm feeling happy for you. You seem like a weight has been lifted off of you and that you are at least enjoying the possibility of being with Adam."

Smiling bashfully, Mia began to come clean about her thoughts and feelings. "I can't lie, Brook. I am a little excited at the prospect of being intimate with Adam. It's been so long since

I've been touched in a sexual manner by anyone. David and I lost that connection a long time ago. Now, here is Adam looking at me with passion in his eyes, letting me know that he desires me, that he wants me. And as we know, everyone wants to be wanted."

"That I know for sure. And you are more than worthy of not only being desired but of being loved. I want you to experience the kind of love that completely consumes you, leaves you wanting for nothing."

"I don't know, Brook, that sounds like a fantasy. I find it hard to believe that that kind of love really exists. The only all consuming love that I've ever known of was for and from God."

"I know that it may be a little hard for you to imagine right now, but Mia, God can bring that kind of love into your life in the form of a companion. I'm telling you what I know."

"Well, be thankful, Brook. There aren't many other people that can honestly say that they have known that kind of love."

"I am lucky, and you will be too."

They continued to shop for lingerie a while longer and then moved on to explore other stores. It was a great afternoon of laughing, sharing, and shopping. It seemed like it had been months since the friends had been able to enjoy one another's company the way that they were today. There were no confrontations, no hurt feelings, and absolutely no talk about Tameka Williams.

Mia waited anxiously for Adam to arrive. They had decided to go to the High Museum of Art for the monthly mixer followed by dinner at Morton's. Checking herself in the mirror one last time, Mia smiled and was pleased with the woman looking back at her. A moment later, the doorbell rang, and Mia smoothed her dress, checked her profile one last time and headed for the door.

They arrived at the museum, secured a couple of drinks and began a self guided tour. The atmosphere was so laid back and relaxing. Mia found herself gently swaying to the soft jazz being played in the background. Adam was simply enjoying the scenery, and that scenery for him was Mia.

"Why are you looking at me like that?" Mia asked softly.

"I'm sorry. Am I making you uncomfortable?"

"No, not at all. Just wondering what you were thinking."

Adam leaned back a little and smiled. "I was thinking about how gorgeous you are and how lucky I am to be here with you."

"Thank you," Mia blushed.

They continued their tour, and as they walked, Adam found himself gently taking Mia's hand in his. As soon as he touched her, butterflies invaded her stomach. Mia was trying so hard to be strong and resist the temptation of being intimate with Adam, but the electricity between them was undeniable. They finished their drinks and their tour and decided to leave so that they'd have time to make their dinner reservation. As they walked out of the museum doors hand in hand, they came face to face with David, Willow and Wayne.

David stopped dead in his tracks. "So, I see you didn't waste any time hooking up with the hired help."

"Better that I hook up with him than with someone who has the same equipment as I do," Mia shot back.

"And I assume that this little partnership has been going on for some time. So you took my daughter from me because of my bad behavior, and all the while you were fucking someone else."

"You know what David, screw you. I was true to my marriage vows. I was faithful in every way. It was you who was creeping and doing so with another dude no less. You freaking fag," Mia growled through clenched teeth.

David immediately lunged towards Mia with a rage she remembered all too well. But before he could reach her, Adam stepped forward and dared David to touch her. "I would hate to have to kill you tonight, but I will." Adam's words were stern, and David knew that Adam meant what he'd said. Without giving David a chance to respond, Wayne stepped forward and grabbed David by the arm. "Come on man, let's just go." Wayne pleaded.

"Yeah, David, go on and go with your boyfriend," Mia retorted. Then she took Adam's hand and they proceeded to walk away. They could still hear David shouting obscenities as they got in the car and drove away.

"Are you okay?" Adam asked.

"Yes, I'm alright," Mia replied with tears running down her face. "Well, maybe I'm not okay. I hate to ruin our evening, but do you mind if we pass on Morton's?"

"Not at all. I'll take you home and let you have a chance to collect yourself. We can always pick this date up at another time."

"No!" Mia exclaimed.

"No, you don't want to go out at a later date?"

"Yes, of course we can go out again, but I'm not ready for this date to end."

Adam caught himself smiling, glad that he'd have more time with Mia. "What do you say we stop and pick up a bite to eat and head on over to your house?"

"That sounds like a plan," Mia sighed.

Forty-five minutes later, they walked into the house with a sack full of burritos, chips, and salsa from Moe's. Mia excused herself and went to change into something a little less dressy and a lot more comfortable. While in her bedroom, she could hear Adam goofing around with the CD player. She was pleased to hear Nina Simone's unmistakable voice fill the air. There was nothing as good as classic jazz, and Nina did it best. Mia finished dressing and returned to Adam's side. He looked at her and smiled sweetly. Mia set the table, lit the candles, poured the wine and they sat down to eat.

"You have a great music collection going on there," Adam commented.

"Music is very important to me. It's an amazing form of expression. I tend to get so caught up in the words and the emotion of the music."

"I know what you mean. Some of it can really speak to your soul." The conversation continued to flow as they munched on their dinner. A little while later, they took their wine glasses and retired to the family room. They sat on the couch, a little closer to one another than Mia had intended for them be, but she made no effort to put more distance between them. When the song *Wild Is the Wind* began to play, Mia got very quiet.

"Is everything okay?" Adam asked softly.

"This song is heart wrenching. She is describing a love so powerful and so all consuming. I used to think that I shared that kind of love with someone, but as time went on, I realized that I've never known anything like that and probably never will. As beautiful and dramatic as it is, it now has a tendency to make me a little sad."

"Why don't we try and turn that around?" Adam stood to his feet and held his hand out for Mia. She accepted his hand as he helped her to her feet. He took her in his arms, and they danced. Their bodies pressed closely together. Mia's head rested on Adam's shoulder, and she drank in his scent. Her sadness was replaced by feelings of comfort and security. She felt so safe in Adam's arms.

The song came to an end, and Adam relaxed his hold on Mia. He took a small step back and gazed at her with so much affection in his eyes. Mia no longer had the strength or desire to fight against what she knew she wanted, and what she wanted was to be made love to. Mia returned his gaze and then leaned in for a kiss. Adam brought his hand up to Mia's face and caressed it in his palm while kissing her gently. But soon, the gentle kiss began to get stronger and more passionate. Their breath quickened and Mia could feel Adam's excitement growing.

"Mia, you know that I want you, but I don't want you doing

anything that you're not ready for. I'm more than happy to wait for you."

Mia took Adam by the hand and led him down the hall to her bedroom. "Adam, I want you to make love to me. I am ready to be with you." Adam kissed her once again and began to remove her clothes. He gently laid Mia on the bed and kissed every inch of her body. He entered her lovingly, and they shared an amazing night of passion.

# CHAPTER FORTY-TWO

Time and love were healing the wounds left by David. Mia was happy and peaceful, and Kaylie was thriving and loving her little life. Mia's only wish now was for Brook to regain her inner peace. Ever since the kidnapping incident, Brook seemed angry and bitter all the time. She had zero tolerance for anything that wasn't just as she wanted it. Her patience level was shot. The only ones that seemed to catch a break from her were her kids. But it was Mia and Eric's hope that the events planned for the day would help to turn Brook's attitude around.

Mia had finished redecorating her home and had decided to host a barbeque. She wanted everything to be festive and fun for everybody, especially Brook. In addition to Brook, Eric, and the kids, Adam would be there as well as a few other couples. Kaylie was excited about it all because she was expecting a few friends and there would be a couple of moonwalks set up in the backyard for the kid's enjoyment. Kaylie was determined to help Mia with all the preparations, and Mia just didn't have the heart to tell her that she was a little in the way.

"Mommy, where does this go?" Kaylie asked rather loudly.

"That goes on the long table outside, baby." Mia looked at her run off and wished for half of the energy that Kaylie had.

"Mommy, where do you want me to put this?" Kaylie shouted more enthusiastically than she did the first time.

"Umm, you can sit that on the kitchen table for me."

"Okay. There are some more groceries in that bag, Mommy. What do you want me to do with them?"

"You know what Kaylie, how about you go to your room and make sure that everything is clean and that your games are set up for you and your friends."

"That's a good idea, Mommy. I want everything to be just right when they get here." Kaylie went skipping off, satisfied that she had an important job to do. Mia, on the other hand, breathed a slight sigh of relief because she would have a few moments without questions.

It was still a couple of hours before the guests would start to arrive, but Mia was expecting Brook to show up a little early. Not that Mia needed any help. She was hoping to have a little time before-hand to speak to Brook about the anger she'd been harboring. Brook had always been so loving and forgiving; that's the Brook that Eric and Mia wanted to see re-emerge. Mia tried to put herself in Brook's place and could only imagine how Brook must feel after everything that had transpired. How could anyone cope with the knowledge that some crazed fool tried to kidnap their baby and that their mortal enemy was the one that saved them from only God knows what?

The sound of the doorbell snatched Mia out of her momentary trance. She went and flung the door open. "Hey, Brook. You're here earlier than I thought you'd be. Where's the rest of your crew?"

"The kids are going to ride over with Eric a little later."

"Well, you know the routine. Come on in and roll your sleeves up."

Brook followed Mia through the house and into the kitchen. Brook washed her hands and started chopping the onions and peppers for the baked beans. "So, you want to tell me about your date the other week?" Brook quizzed with a sly grin.

"It, of course, started off wonderfully. But as we were leaving the museum, it took an ugly turn."

With her curiosity running wild, Brook asked, "What in the world went wrong?"

"As we were walking out, David, Wayne, and Willow were walking in. Then David accused me of being involved with Adam the entire time we were separated. Can you believe the nerve of him?"

"Please tell me that you and Adam just kept walking and ignored his ass."

"Not quite." Mia admitted. "I said some ugly things, one of which I really regret. I told him that at least I was with someone of the opposite sex, and then, Brook, I called him a fag."

Brook burst into laughter. "What did he say to that? Man I wish I could've seen the expression on his face."

"Brook, he was furious. He actually lunged towards me."

"He didn't put his hands on you, did he?"

"No, Adam stepped to him to let him know that there wouldn't be any of that. But the thing I hated the most was that I called him such a derogatory name. Brook, you know that I have gay friends that I adore. I would never want to do or say anything that would cause them any pain."

"Honey, your friends would understand. What that man put you through was unfathomable."

"Yeah, but that's still no excuse. We would never accept that if one of our Caucasian friends used the 'N' word."

"Well I'm sorry, Mia. I don't care what anyone says, being gay is not the same as being African American. Their struggles are just not the same."

"The struggles may not be the same, but we do have to recognize that there are struggles. I think that's one of the reasons that gay men find it so hard to come out and be their true selves. I mean look at David, he's ready to kill anyone that calls him gay. In his twisted mind, sexual activity with a man is just a fetish. As long as he's the giver and not the receiver, he doesn't consider himself gay or even bisexual."

"Then that just makes him a fool who's living in a constant state of denial," Brook retorted. "Now back to the date."

"You're a mess. Anyway, after our little encounter, I was in no mood to go out to eat. Adam was so sweet and understanding. We ended up swinging by Moe's of all places and grabbing some food to go. We came back over here, nibbled at our food, and enjoyed the rest of the evening."

"Mia, are you telling me that nothing else happened?"

"I'm telling you that it was an amazing night." Mia began to giggle like a school girl. "For the first time in over a year, a man touched me, spoke to me, caressed me, and made love to me like I was the only one in the world he wanted. Until it happened, I never knew how much I missed a man's hands."

"Wow! I'm glad for you girl. You held out a long time. In the midst of all that pain and anguish that David was causing you, you stayed faithful and true. You deserve to be happy and loved."

"Yeah, I do." Mia walked over to the stereo and turned the music up a little. She danced back into the kitchen and continued preparing the deviled eggs. After a couple of minutes passed, Mia worked up the nerve to bring up Brooks latest emotional struggles. "So Brook, how have you been? Are you dealing any better with the emotional fallout from the attempted kidnapping?"

"I don't think that you and Eric really get it. That man had every intention of killing my baby. I'm sure of it. And while I am so thankful to God for sparing her life, I'm also convinced that Tameka also planned to hurt my child. Knowing that, it's hard to fall over myself praising her for the bravery she displayed."

"That's just it, Brook. Eric does get it. It was his child that was in danger too. And what you don't realize is how much guilt Eric has been carrying around." Mia spoke with pleading eyes, trying to make Brook understand how Eric was feeling.

"What are you talking about, Mia. What does he have to feel guilty about?"

"Eric somehow has it in his head that if he'd been in town none of this would've happened. He thinks that his excessive travel left you all vulnerable. He's been beating himself up since all of this happened. So yes, Brook, he gets it."

"I...I didn't know he felt that way. Eric has always been there for us. There is no way that he could have prevented any of that mess."

"I hate to tell you, Brook, but you've been walking around snapping at everybody and always in such a foul mood that he hasn't felt like he's been able to talk to you about the way that either of you have been feelings. You guys really need each other."

"I thought he knew that I needed him."

"Yeah, well he needs you too, Brook."

"I'm doing the best I can, Mia. I just need a little more time."

"Just don't leave your man out there suffering by himself too long, Brook. He loves you with everything he's got. It's your turn to shoulder some of his burden. Y'all have to carry the fall out from all of this together."

The doorbell rang, and while Mia went to greet her guest, Brook went to the restroom to wipe the tears from her face and collect herself. Brook stood in front of the mirror and gazed at her reflection. Mia was right; she had been selfish. Eric needed her just as she had needed him. She would have to find a way to start chipping away at the anger she'd cloaked herself in. Brook returned to the kitchen, determined to at least enjoy the day without a single thought of Tameka or the pervert that snatched her daughter.

The barbeque was, without a doubt, the best idea Mia had come up with in a long time. The kids were running wild in the back yard and bouncing around in the moonwalks like little jumping beans. The adults were all engaged in conversations that ranged from parenthood to politics. The music was good, and the food was great. Even Brook seemed to be enjoying herself. It was the first time in a long time that she laughed out loud and appeared to be completely worry free.

By seven o'clock, the guests were starting to leave and Mia and Adam were starting to clear away some of the mess. Brook and Eric were in the back room with the kids putting in a movie so that they could settle down and hopefully drift off until it was time to leave.

"Alright, Adam, I'm giving you a reprieve. I'll finish this up with Mia, and you can go hang out with Eric," Brook offered.

Adam looked at Mia as if to ask "Is it okay?" Mia gave him a peck and sent him on his way. The two women went about the business of cleaning up and talking and laughing about the events of the day. The doorbell rang and Mia dried her hands as she walked to answer it. She couldn't imagine who it could be; all of the invited guests had come, enjoyed themselves, and left. "Oh no," was all that Mia could manage to say. Standing on the other side of the door was Tameka. Just as Mia swung the door open, Brook turned the corner and asked bitterly, "What the hell is she doing here?"

"Mia, I'm sorry to intrude, but would you mind if I came in for a minute? I have information that I think you all would want to hear."

"Mia, she has nothing to say that I care to hear. Don't you dare let her in here," Brook screamed. The volume and pitch of her voice drew Eric and Adam in from the backyard. Eric stepped to Brook's side hoping to try and calm her down.

"Look everybody, I'm not here to cause any trouble. Brook, as angry as you are, I know that you'll want to hear what I have to say." Tameka was practically pleading with Brook.

"Come on in, Tameka." Mia stepped to the side to allow her enough room to enter into the house.

"What the hell?" Brook screeched in disbelief.

"Baby, lets just hear what she has to say," Eric encouraged.

"Come on everyone; let's go talk in the kitchen." Mia closed the door and started walking towards the kitchen hoping that everyone, including Brook, would follow. Mia, Brook, and Tameka took a seat while the men chose to stand. "Okay, Tameka, what is it that you need to share with us?" Mia asked.

"First, I'd like to thank Brook and Eric for the kind words spoken at the press conference. I know that it was difficult to say the things that you did, Eric. Secondly, I'd like to apologize to you guys. Yes, I was the one that took your daughter out of harm's way, but truth be told, that was not my original plan. I had every intention of using her as a means to scare you. I was not going to harm her. I had actually planned fun activities for the afternoon. Your daughter would have enjoyed herself, but I would have accomplished my mission of scaring you, Brook."

"But why, Tameka? What would have been the point of that?" Brook hissed.

"You know what? The rational was stupid and doesn't even matter now. What counts is that while witnessing the kidnapping, I had an epiphany. I realized that I had been placed in the position to choose good over evil. I could instantly choose to become a better person than what I had been in the past. Being there for your little girl has completely changed the way that I see myself and what I envision for my future."

Brook didn't know why, but something told her that Tameka was speaking from her heart and telling the truth. Everyone expected Brook to attack Tameka, but instead, she seemed to relax and melt into her seat. All of the anger and resentment started to drain from her body.

"Brook, Eric, I can't apologize enough for the pain I caused you all in the past. I am so very sorry. And I've made a decision that I think will give you both a new level of comfort and give me the chance to really start over. I'm moving to Houston, Texas next week."

Confused, Brook questioned Tameka about her pending

move. "How are you going to do that, Tameka? I didn't think that you could leave the state while on parole."

"Normally you can't, but because of my circumstance, I've been granted special permission."

"And what circumstance is that?" Mia questioned.

"I've been offered a new anchor position with a Houston station. It's a great opportunity, and it frees you all from worrying about having me around."

"How does Wayne feel about this move?" Mia asked gently.

"Well, Mia, unlike David, Wayne has come completely clean and now owns his homosexuality. He doesn't think that David ever will. He says that David's too afraid of the stigma attached to gay men. I personally think that he's still deep in a state of denial."

"Humph. No question about that." Mia shook her head in disgust.

"Okay, that's all I came to say. I wish all of you only the best."

"Will you be back to testify against the man that kidnapped our girl?" Eric questioned.

"Oh my goodness, I can't believe I forgot to tell y'all. He was the main reason I came over here. I thought I'd conduct a little investigation of this guy. It turns out that he had served time before on rape and kidnapping charges. He'd been in trouble with the law since he was fourteen years old. Because of his criminal history, a conviction on the kidnapping of Kristen would guarantee him life in prison without the possibility of parole. I guess that was unacceptable for him. One of my sources told me that he was found dead in his cell this morning. He hung himself. It'll be all over the news by tonight."

Brook burst into tears. "Oh my God! It's all over, it's really over." Eric went to his wife's side and took her in his arms. Everyone that had caused them fear and pain was now out of their lives for good. While everyone rejoiced over the news,

Tameka quietly showed herself out. She took a good look around, absorbing the beauty of the evening. Tameka took a deep breath, gave herself a pat on the back and then she was gone.

# ACKNOWLEDGMENTS

I would like to first and foremost thank God for everything and everyone that He has placed in my life. I'm thankful for every lesson and blessing. His goodness is endless. Thank you to my family for their continuous love and support. Ken and Joshua, you guys are amazing, and Joshua, thank you for telling any and every one you encounter that your mom is an author.

Thank you, Myrt (Mommy) for consistently being a source of love and encouragement. A special thanks to Cassandra Smith for giving me the encouragement to start this journey and for your never ending support and friendship. Last but certainly not least, thank you to everyone that took the time to read my work. Your support means everything.

## ALSO BY STACEY COVINGTON-LEE

The Knife In My Back

Bitter Taste Of Love

Hate The Way He Loves Me

When Love Ain't Enough

The Love That Lies Between Us

Coming summer 2019, her much anticipated novel, He Won't Go.

For bookings please email inquires@staceycovingtonlee.com.